INTERNATIONAL BESTSELLING AUTHOR

KATEMARIE COLLINS

Consort of the Successor

Cover Art:
Streganova Designs

Publisher's Note:

This is a work of fiction. All names, characters, places, and events are the work of the author's imagination.

Any resemblance to real persons, places, or events is coincidental.

Solstice Publishing - www.solsticepublishing.com

Consort of the Successor

A Novel of Tiadar

By

KateMarie Collins

For Melissa Pollotta

For the best Friday the 13th EVER

Chapter One

"Talin, stop pacing. You're making me nervous." Kade laughed, not entirely in jest.

Talin stopped. Reaching his hand up to his collar, he tugged at it. Not that it was tight or constrictive, but out of a need to do something with his hands. "Well, you're used to all of…*this*." He waved his hands over the blue and silver uniform he wore. Royal colors. He'd been a member of the Royal Guard for as long as he could remember. The colors weren't new. The regal cut of them, and what was about to happen, were.

Kade leaned back in his chair, one arm draped against the back of the empty seat next to him. His uniform was only marginally more ornate than Talin's. "Oh, come on. It's not that bad. You did agree to this, you know." His friend's face got serious. "You're not regretting that, are you?"

Taking a deep breath, he replied, "No. Not one bit. I'll do whatever Lily asks of me. Even if it means ruling at her side. That's not the hard part."

"Then what's the problem?" Kade asked, exasperated.

"You're going to laugh at me." Talin moved to a chair on the other side and dropped to the seat. He raked one hand through his red hair and didn't look at his friend.

"I promise not to."

"It's that everyone's going to be looking at me. I'm not used to being the center of attention." A muffled chuckle came from Kade. Talin's head shot up and he glared at his oldest friend. "You promised!" he accused, pointing a finger at him.

"I'm sorry, I didn't mean to." Kade's attempts to hide his amusement were failing. "Try this. Ignore everyone in the room but Lily. Given that it's her coronation as heir as well, she's going to be scrutinized just as bad, or worse, than you are. Show her she made the right choice in you as her consort. Lend her your strength, even if you're an absolute mess inside."

A thought struck Talin. "Is that how you're getting through your wedding vows?" He smiled as Kade's eyes started to shift and looked away at the wall.

"Yeah, well. That's different."

Talin laughed, "Of course it is," he replied.

A door on one side of the room opened. Talin leapt to his feet, his hands automatically tugging on the bottom of his jacket to make sure it fit correctly and wasn't rumpled. A side effect of years in the guard, he knew, but now he took comfort in the gesture. *You're getting a promotion,* he told himself, *that's all. A really big one, sure, but the ceremony won't be that different. I hope.*

Corvin, Kade's father and the current King of Tiadar, strode into the room and shut the door behind him. The crown worn by the ruling Consort sat on his brow. Keryth ran things, and Corvin supported her in every way he could. That was how it would be with Talin and Lily. And, if he was going to be honest with himself, he was glad for that. He loved Lily with all his soul. But he would've been hopeless as king.

"I think they're about ready out there. How about you two?" Corvin asked.

Kade answered, "I'm fine. That one," he pointed a finger at Talin, "is a nervous wreck. Lily might have to hold him upright to finish things."

Talin swatted Kade's hand away, "Traitor," he joked. Turning his attention back to Corvin, he said, "I'm ready." He released a deep breath and knew he spoke the truth. No matter what, he was doing this. For Lily, and the promise of a future with her.

"Good," Corvin nodded slightly. "You remember everything from the rehearsal yesterday?"

"Yes, I think so. You and Her Majesty go first. Kade and I come out, followed by Lily and Rylin. I stand with Lily, say the oath when directed, and do my best not to fall over." He smiled at the last.

The King smiled back. "That last bit's important. You don't want to pass out like I did. Had a headache for three days from my head hitting the step." He reached out and placed a hand on Talin's shoulder. "I'm glad she chose you, Talin. Keryth and I have long considered you part of our family, not just one of our guards. You'll be able to help Lily in the days and years ahead in a way we can't. Thank you for that. Your mother would've been proud to see the man you've become."

The sincerity in the older man's voice touched Talin deeply. "Thank you, sir. That means a lot to me," he said, his voice quiet.

Trumpets blared a fanfare, signaling the start of the processional. Corvin dropped his arm back to his side. "Well, that's our cue." He opened the door and stood aside, waiting.

Taking a deep breath, Talin stepped out into the antechamber that led to the main throne room. Keryth stood, tall and regal. There was no sign of Lily or Rylin.

As Corvin strode to take Keryth's arm, Talin took his place behind the king. After all, when the day came that Lily ruled, his role would still be consort over ruler. *Let that day be decades away*, he prayed. The tall, ornate double doors parted and the royal couple began their walk to the thrones at the opposite end.

"Remember," Kade kept his voice low. "This is about Lily more than you. And she's going to be even more terrified than you are. You and I can open a bottle later tonight, and I can listen to how frightened this makes you. But she needs your strength now."

Talin nodded his understanding. Kade was right, and he knew it. Lily had grown so much since her return to Tiadar a year ago, most in the months that followed her confirmation. There were signs of the abuse she suffered at Erena's hands still present, but she was becoming more at ease with her true self. That inner strength he loved so much in her had begun to blossom. But elaborate ceremonies like this, where she was on display, would test that resolve.

The music sounded once again, signaling the two of them to start their own long march forward. As he emerged from the shadowy recesses of the antechamber, Talin was struck by the sheer number of people filling the audience chamber itself. He'd been in it several times, as royal guard or simply to marvel at the carved arches and painted glass, but had never seen it filled to capacity.

"Viewing balcony's full, too," Kade commented, keeping his head facing forward. "Don't look. You won't see anyone and you're supposed to focus on Their Majesties anyway. At least, until Lily arrives."

"How do you know it's full, then?" Quickly, Talin did the math. If the balcony was full, the chamber was close to a thousand faces. Not all of which would be friendly ones.

"Grayson let me know early this morning. So many folk showed up yesterday, hoping for the chance to glimpse the proceedings, Her Majesty ordered coins to be handed out. Those lucky enough to get one were granted admittance to the balcony."

Talin whispered, "Sounds like something your mother would do."

"She'll be your mother soon enough, you know. Or, at least, mother-in-law."

Talin didn't dare respond as they'd reached the bottom of the dais. Three steps up to the thrones. Keryth and Corvin sat, their faces impassive, in the center. Two smaller seats, one on each side, awaited him and Lily. A circlet, nothing more than silver wire woven in a simple pattern, sat on each padded seat.

Bowing deeply, Talin shifted to his left. Kade stood near him. In rehearsal, he'd remarked about how the placement felt more like a wedding than coronation. It was Keryth's reply that struck him the most.

It is a wedding of sorts. You are not marrying each other. Not yet, anyway. But you are committing yourselves to the kingdom. To the people of Tiadar. Those vows are no less sacred than what is exchanged between two individuals.

The music changed. Instead of trumpets blaring, notes from a dozen harps cascaded from the hidden recesses scattered around the chamber. Talin shifted his attention to the chamber he had left.

Lily emerged, Rylin just slightly behind her. Something jabbed his ribs. "Breathe," Kade ordered. Talin did as he was told, but couldn't tear his gaze off of Lily.

Her black hair was swept off her face, the green eyes serious. He could see a slight twitch to her eyebrow. She was nervous, just like he was. Her dress, silver lace over a deep sapphire blue, was unlike anything Talin had seen before. Instead of the high waist favored by most women in the kingdom, it fit closely to her waist before falling gracefully into a full skirt.

"Damn it, Lily." Kade muttered under his breath.

Without turning, Talin whispered back, "What's wrong?"

"The dress. I know she said she wanted something a little different. She's going to have every person that can work with needle and thread trying to put that design out now. Rylin's in love with it. I can see it on her face."

"What's wrong with that?"

"Cost, Talin. It's going to be expensive."

Talin bit his cheek to keep from laughing. Lily and Rylin made it to the edge of the dais. Shifting, he took his place next to her.

What happened next was a blur. Oaths were said, promises made. Keryth placed a circlet on Lily's head first. Corvin handed the other one to Lily while Talin knelt in front of her. The metal fit his brow perfectly. Then they were allowed to take their seats next to the king and queen. Kade moved forward, taking Rylin's hand, and were the first to pledge their loyalty to the Heir and her Consort.

Once that was done, Kade moved behind Talin's seat while Rylin settled behind Lily. "At least you get to sit down for the rest of this," he muttered. "My feet are going to be killing me by the time we get to the banquet."

Talin stopped trying to remember the names and faces after the first half hour. Some were noticeably absent. A representative of Heren's house came, muttered the oath under his breath, and all but ran from Keryth's glare. Heren resided in solitary exile, a man alone on an island that no shadrim could reach. Jasper, while not in exile, was under house arrest. His every move was documented and reported back to the Crown. Everyone in his employ had scattered to different residences.

For her part in everything, Erena was locked in a cell. Where, exactly, Talin didn't know. Lily had asked her mother to spare the woman's life. Not out of compassion, but so she could spend her days seeing the damage she did to Lily unravel. The harshest punishment would be for her to see Lily rule as Queen in her own right and not the puppet for another.

"Any word on your cousin yet?" Talin muttered to Kade.

"No." Kade put a great deal of vehemence in that single word.

Iris was the only one they hadn't found. She'd kept out of the council chamber during the presentation. She'd fled after Lily proved that she could not just do a little bit of magic. The truth had come out at last. S*he must've known it was possible*, Talin reasoned. *It's the only logical reason why she didn't attend. Iris never was stupid. If she thought there was even a chance Lily would expose everyone and their plots against her, she would've run.*

At last, the line was dwindling. A lone figure approached the thrones. There was something familiar about his face, but the man's hood obscured some of his features. The plain gray and brown of his outfit was both unremarkable and unmistakable at the same time.

One of the royal guard stepped forward. "Sir, it is customary to remove your hood when approaching Their Majesties and Their Heirs."

The man raised a single hand and pushed back his hood. A shock of red hair, unkempt and bushy, erupted from his head. He turned and looked right at Talin.

"Hello, son."

Chapter Two

Talin sat in his chair, stunned. A movement to his left caught his eye. Glancing her way, he saw Lily looking at him, curiosity on her face. She formed a circle with her thumb and forefinger. Their signal that the other was open to using the mental link they shared since the day he touched the Mark on her neck with her permission. Keryth had summoned Grayson to her side and was whispering something to him.

Nodding slightly to Lily, he let his mind open up. Her voice echoed in his head. *"Talin, is he your father?"*

"I don't know," he replied. *"Mom never talked about him. Only said he was gone. I thought that meant he was dead."*

Keryth stood, and Talin scrambled to his feet as the rest rose with her. "This is not the place or time for a reunion, sir. There are other duties and obligations which the Heir and her Consort must fulfill yet. Please accompany Grayson. He will see to your needs and find you a place at the banquet. We will make sure you and Talin have time tomorrow to speak."

The disheveled man smiled. Something in his face made Talin cautious of his motives, but he couldn't place what. "Of course, Your Majesty." He bowed and followed Grayson out of the room. Three other guards followed behind.

Keryth turned her gaze to Talin. "Later," she commanded. Turning her attention back to the crowd, she addressed them. "The Heir and her Consort have heard your oaths and made theirs to you. May the day never come that those words are tested." She held out a hand to Corvin and the two began to process out of the room.

Talin stood and moved down the steps, meeting Lily in the middle, and took her hand. *"I don't know who he is,"* he sent to her. *"I'm sorry he interrupted your coronation, though."*

"He certainly woke me up," she sent back. *"I was falling asleep up there during the presentations. Rylin had to keep nudging me."*

They met Keryth and Corvin in the antechamber. The Queen held up a hand as Talin drew a breath. "Not yet, Talin," she commanded. "When Kade and Rylin join us, and we're alone, then we'll discuss this development."

Talin nodded. Lily squeezed his hand in reassurance. "She sent Grayson with him. He'll report back before you have to meet him," she whispered.

Lily was right. Grayson was one of Talin's closest friends in the Guard. The older man had acted like a father to him for most of his life, guiding him through the ranks, encouraging him to improve his fighting. Indeed, the only thing that drove him more than Lily was trying to best Kade.

They waited in silence until the doors closed behind Kade and Rylin. Keryth removed her crown and handed it to one of her attendants. "Lily, you and Talin should keep yours on until after the banquet," she instructed. Turning her attention to Talin, she spoke again. "I don't know who this man is. Do you?"

"No, I don't. Mom always told me my father was gone. I took it to mean dead." Talin took a deep breath. "That he shows up, here, today…I haven't exactly been shy, Your Majesty. I've travelled with Kade or as part of the royal progress around the country for years. I find it odd that he'd show up like this." He met Keryth's gaze. "After what happened in the council at Lily's confirmation…I simply don't trust anyone beyond this room. He could be anyone, sent by anybody."

"Like Iris." Keryth nodded. "I appreciate your caution, Talin. But we can't keep him at arm's length for long. He'll be at the banquet, but I instructed that it be at one of the far tables. He'll be able to see you, and will be watched. Grayson will assess him, find out if he is who he says he is. I should have that report in the morning. Then, and only then, will I let you two meet." She paused, "If he truly is your father, and I hope he is, you will have a long road ahead of you. It will be your decision how much of your life you want him to be part of. It won't be easy, either."

"I understand."

She nodded, and turned to Lily. "You need to stay clear of this man," she commanded. "Until we know more. Please."

"I plan to." Lily looked up at Talin. He saw concern in her eyes. "Talin, I hope he's your father. I really do. But something about him troubles me. Anyone that walks away from a child and shows up when things are going well has a reason for it. Like you said, you haven't been hidden away. Not like I was. People know who you are. He could've found you years ago. Why today?"

He put his arms around her and pulled her close, loving the feel of her cheek as it pressed against his chest. "Don't worry, Lily. Whatever he really wants, he won't get it."

As he spoke the words, he tried to quell the unease he felt. His mother never said his father was dead. To be honest, he couldn't remember a time she'd said much about him at all. Only that he was gone before she moved to the city. It was pure luck that she found a job within the royal household and Talin had been able to grow up as he did. He didn't remember anything beyond life in court, the guard. Kade was only a year or two older than he was, and they had been friends longer than Talin could remember. Briefly, after his mother died, he thought about trying to find out if there were more relatives out there. Were his mother's parents still living and he should tell them? The only person who could answer that question, though, had passed away. She gave him a good life, one he was grateful for, but the curiosity began to rise again. Could this vagabond really be his father?

If so, why wait until now to come forward?

His stomach rumbled, reminding him he'd not eaten since breakfast. It was approaching dinnertime now. A wave of weariness passed over him. Talin felt someone's gaze resting on him. Looking up, he locked eyes with Keryth. Her face was calm, impassive. But calculating at the same time. "You'll get used to it, Talin," she remarked. "You need to think about getting a few attendants of your own. People you trust, who'll make sure you eat. Kade, I know you're heading up Lily's security team. Talk with Talin, give him some recommendations." She paused, "Unless you think you can handle both of them."

"I don't understand, Your Majesty. Why would I need any attendants?" Talin asked, confused.

Keryth crossed the small space between them and reached up to touch the silver circlet that still rested on his head. He'd forgotten it was there. "Whether or not you and Lily ever wed, you will rule at her side. Like it or not, Talin, you are now royalty. And appearances must be maintained." A small smile grew on her face as the realization hit home.

She turned away from him and started to talk about the banquet ahead. But he didn't hear much of what she said. Her last few words resounded in his head, burning into his very soul. *You always knew that it was part of all of this*, he chided himself. *Why the shock now? Just because it was finally said out loud? What did you think those people who lined up and swore an oath to you were thinking? They weren't looking at some orphan that got lucky and became part of the Royal Guard. They saw the man that would one day be their king. How or why you got here doesn't matter. It may not be what you planned, but it's the hand you've been dealt. Time to start taking the role seriously.* Taking a deep breath, Talin straightened his stance.

Keryth glanced back at them, one hand resting on top of Corvin's. "It's a start," she said to him, her tone approving.

Holding out his arm, he waited for Lily to join him. They fell into step behind the King and Queen down the corridor that led to the banquet hall. For the first time since Lily asked him to be her Consort, he was keenly aware of the staff as they stopped what they were doing and bowed. True, he'd been part of the inner circle for most of his life. Keryth long since ordered him to stop genuflecting except for formal occasions. Kade once challenged him to a fight if he ever did it to him again. Talin took the time to see the faces as they strode past. Most showed love and respect for them. Old friends smiled a little, happy for him. Some, though, looked angry. He knew their names. He hadn't made it up the ranks in the guard without stepping on a few toes, or egos. Most likely, those people would see this latest promotion as undeserved.

"I see them, Talin," Kade whispered. "Don't worry. They won't make it on the team I'll create for you. They may end up being reassigned to a different job."

Talin nodded once, signaling his understanding. Lily's hand grasped his a little tighter. He glanced her way, smiling, "It's fine," he reassured her.

The massive doors at the end of the hallway opened as they approached. Music filtered in from the room, announcing their entrance. The hall was filled to capacity. Long tables and benches encircled the room. At the far end, on a raised platform, sat a table and chairs for the six of them. Livered attendants stood behind each chair, ready to make sure their every need was met.

Talin tried to keep his focus on the high table. A movement caught the corner of his vision, though, and he glanced over. The man who claimed to be his father bowed as they walked past. The smirk he'd had during the ceremony was still present on his face. *Whatever he wanted to gain from coming forward,* Talin thought, *probably won't be something I'll agree with.* The unease he'd felt when he first saw the man was still there. It would be a long time before Talin would trust him. Even longer before he'd call him father. If ever.

He stopped at the base of the platform while Keryth and Corvin moved to the chairs at the center. He and Lily both bowed to the Queen and King. Talin turned to Lily, bowed again, and kissed her hand before releasing it. He then climbed the short few steps at the end of the table to stand next to Corvin, while Lily followed a similar path opposite of him to end up next to Keryth.

Once Kade and Rylin had taken their places, Keryth raised a single hand. The music stopped, and every person turned to look at her. "Today, the succession has been confirmed. The one who bears the Mark," she gestured at Lily, "has chosen her Consort." Her other hand moved toward Talin. "Long may their future be one of peace and harmony."

"Good health and prosperity," the crowd answered in unison.

Keryth and Corvin sat, signaling Talin he could do the same. The array of silverware and dishes in front of him presented a new challenge. "I thought you were joking," he muttered at Kade.

"About what?" Kade asked as he reached for a goblet filled with wine.

"All of this." Talin waved his hand slightly over the elaborate setting.

"You'll get used to it. Lily did. Just watch me or my dad if you're not sure which one to use. He's an old pro at formal dinners."

Talin nodded. A bowl of soup was placed in front of him. With what he hoped was a sly glance, Talin took note of which spoon Corvin used and began to eat.

They were on the main course when Kade spoke again. "Have you decided what you'll call them?"

"Huh?" Talin responded, confused.

"My parents. Once you and Lily get married, you can hardly call them 'Your Majesty' when we're alone."

Talin choked on the water he was trying to drink. Coughing, he shot a dirty look at Kade.

His friend smiled at him. "Figured you could use something else to think about," was all he said.

"I've got enough on my plate right now, thanks." Talin responded dryly. "I'd rather find out who that man is," he nodded in the general direction of the line of tables where the stranger sat.

"Agreed. No sense worrying about it tonight, though. Don't forget. You still have to do some dancing before this is all over."

"I'm looking forward to that part, at least."

Once the food was cleared, Talin rose and moved behind the chairs to Lily. He looked over the assembled crowd. They'd noticed his movement, and waited expectantly. "I think we're supposed to dance now," he smiled at her. "If that is acceptable to Her Royal Highness, that is."

Lily blushed. "I'd love to." She rose and led him to the end of the table and down the steps to the dance floor.

The musicians began a slow piece, which was fine with Talin. He placed one hand on the small of her back and held her hand with his other. Together, they began to glide across the floor.

"I don't trust him, Talin," she whispered.

"Trust who?"

"The man who said he's your father." Lily looked up at him. "I really hope this is all true. But"—she hesitated—"The only time I've felt like this is when Heren looked at me. He wants something from you."

He looked into her green eyes, "I'll talk with him tomorrow, send him back to wherever he came from. He won't be here long." He tried to reassure her.

About halfway through the song, more couples came out to dance. Talin kept watch as he twirled Lily about, making sure he knew where the mystery man was. The last thing he wanted to deal with was him to try and cut in on a dance.

By the time the second song was over, though, the man had disappeared.

Escorting Lily back to her seat at the high table, he whispered, "He's left." He held out her chair for her, "Stay here. I'll find out where he went." He placed a soft kiss on the top of her head before heading back to the dance floor to find Kade.

He caught his friend's attention, motioning Kade over his way. When the song finished, Kade and Rylin both came over.

"What's wrong?" Kade asked.

"He left. I don't know where. It was during the last song, when Lily and I were dancing." Talin told him.

Kade nodded, his face growing serious. "I'll find out. Rylin, go stay with Lily. Talin, stay here."

"I know this place as well as you do. I can help." Talin insisted.

Kade held up a hand. "That's not the point, Talin. He's here because of you. And we don't know why. The last thing Lily needs is for you to end up missing."

"I can take care of myself, Kade," he said.

"I know you can. So does she," he inclined his head to Lily. "But we don't know who this man is, what he's capable of. And you're officially the Consort of the Successor now. No more bar brawls, whether you like it or not." Kade took Talin by the shoulders. "Your job is to keep Lily safe. And you can't do that if you're not at her side." He spun Talin around. "Go. Reassure her, keep her from getting too concerned. I'll find him before he can do any harm."

Talin nodded, knowing Kade was right. His job had changed along with his rank. Now he could only stay put and hope the man was found.

Chapter Three

Talin sat, staring blankly at the fire burning in the fireplace. His fingers drummed restlessly on the table next to him. Frustrated, he leapt to his feet and started to pace. It'd been hours since the banquet ended, and not a word from Kade about the man claiming to be his father.

He still wasn't used to the opulence of the rooms he now occupied. To be honest, they were sparse by royal standards. He'd asked the servants to remove some of the more ostentatious paintings and decorative items. Asked that the ornate furniture be replaced with items with cleaner lines—less 'swirly' was the term he'd used. He may be royalty now, but he was a soldier at heart. He didn't need to sleep on silk sheets. Though a private bath was a luxury he was learning to enjoy.

He'd remained at Lily's side for the remainder of the banquet, pretending he wasn't concerned. Accepting the congratulations of several people who approached, making small talk. Goddess, how he'd hated that. Kade had been telling him for years that it was one of the hardest parts of his job, but he'd learned to deal with it. But just how many times could he discuss the wonderful colors on the trees or the crisp air that promised a hard winter before he stopped caring?

Finally, it was over and Keryth and Corvin retired. That made it easier for him to escort Lily back to her rooms. The formal gatherings were even harder on her, and he knew that. She wasn't as withdrawn as she was when she first came back to Tiadar, but that didn't mean she felt completely at ease surrounded by strangers. Especially when most of them wanted something from her.

He strode to the door, one hand going to the handle, and stopped. The door would be guarded; they'd want to know where he was going. Or simply follow him. He lowered his head to rest against the door. He didn't regret a thing where it came to Lily. But he did long for things to be simpler again. *That's not going to happen until after you're married, if that happens,* he told himself. *Until then, every interaction you have with Lily will be watched, analyzed. Okay, so if we were watched and analyzed before I agreed to be her Consort, I just didn't notice it.*

"Talin!" Lily's terrified voice screamed in his head.

His hand leaned on the latch, throwing open the door. Sound assaulted his ears, making them ring, as his arm shielded his face from the debris flying at him.

Staggering, he felt the floor quiver from the force of the blast. He caught sight of the corridor that led away from his rooms collapsing into a pile of rubble. The two guards slumped against the wall next to his door. Kneeling, he checked for their pulses.

"Lily! What happened? Are you okay?" he sent to her.

She didn't answer.

He pulled a handkerchief from a pocket and held it against his mouth and nose to filter out the dust billowing up from the hallway. Spying a torch still burning in a wall sconce, he grabbed it before starting his way down the hallway.

Lily's rooms were closest. Scrambling over larger stones and rubble, he got to the door. The guards, both with blood seeping from wounds to their heads, worked at removing the debris blocking the door.

"Lily!" Talin screamed. "I'm here…We're clearing the door now. Are you okay?"

"Talin?" Her voice was faint.

He bent down and grabbed the rock closest to him and threw it off to the side. "Are you hurt?' he called out.

"We're fine, Talin," Rylin's muffled voice came through the door. "She's scared, though."

He allowed himself a moment to take a breath, grateful that Rylin was in there with her. "Hang on, we're working as fast as we can out here." He kept digging, intent on clearing enough space to swing the door open and get inside.

Others came over. Some helped him dig, while a couple led the injured guards away to be treated. "Has anyone reached Their Majesties?" he demanded.

"The hallway's blocked, but I heard they're alive. It's going to take time to reach them," one of the guardsmen answered

"Check the two guards by my room when you can, please," Talin directed. "They were alive, but down."

"They've been taken care of already."

Kade's response startled Talin. Looking up, he realized his friend was working near him. His dark hair was disheveled, and clothing coated in dust. The shoulder of his jacket was torn at the seam. Something wasn't right.

Kade looked at him, his green eyes guarded. "Not here, not now," he whispered.

Something was beyond not right.

With renewed energy, Talin tackled the dwindling pile of debris blocking the doorway. As he pulled the last few chunks of stone aside, Kade pulled the door open. "Stay here," he commanded the rest of the rescuers before sliding his body through the narrow opening. Talin followed.

Lily sat in a chair on the far side of the room. Her head was in her hands. Her shoulders shook slightly. Rylin knelt in front of her.

Both women raised their heads as they entered. Rylin flew into Kade's arms, but Lily sat there. Talin could see the tears that slowly seeped down her cheeks.

Crossing the room, he knelt in front of her. "Are you okay?" he asked, his voice low.

"Why, Talin?" She choked out.

"Why what? Lily, what happened?" he tried to take her hand, but she pulled away from him.

"She wants to know why you tried to kill her parents, Talin," Rylin said.

Shocked, he sat back. He looked at Lily, then over to Kade and Rylin. "I didn't try to kill anyone. Especially not Their Majesties! I've been in my room since the banquet ended!" He looked back at Lily. "Are they okay?"

"They are. I'd just left them when I found you," Kade's voice had a dangerous edge to it. "They're alive, but hurt."

"We saw you, Talin." Lily's voice was barely above a whisper. "We were leaving their rooms, coming back here. You walked right past me with a package in your hands."

"It wasn't me! I swear…" he looked at the floor, trying to comprehend what they were saying. "Kade, it had to be the strange man from the confirmation. It wasn't me. Didn't you find him after he left the banquet?"

"What man, Talin? Nothing strange happened at the ceremony, or after."

Talin rose from the floor, "You were all there. He was the last one to come up and swear the oath. Claimed he was my father. The Queen had Grayson escort him out, talk to him. He was at the banquet and then disappeared. You had me stay with Lily while you went looking for him." He spoke rapidly, trying to remember everything about the man he remembered. "He was dressed in brown and grey…had his hood up…didn't take it off until told to do so when he approached."

Kade kept his voice low, "Talin, I don't know what you're talking about. The last one during the oath was a guardsman. One from your old unit. His hair's blonde, not red."

Talin's head flew up and he looked right at Kade. "If you never saw him, how'd you know his hair was red? I didn't say that just now."

Kade's face twisted in thought. "I don't know…"

"Are you saying there's someone here that looks like you? And you've met him?" Lily asked.

Talin moved back to her and knelt. "Lily, I did not do this. I know there was someone else here, someone who claimed to be my father. His hair was as red as mine. Was about the same build. I don't know how or why he'd make all of you forget he was here, though."

"To make it look like you did this, that's why." Kade answered.

Talin didn't look at his friend. He kept his focus on Lily. Her tears had stopped. She looked at him, pain and confusion on her face. "I want to believe you, Talin. But we *saw* you…"

"What do you remember after the banquet was over?" Kade asked.

"I walked Lily back here, said goodnight, and went to my rooms. And waited for you, Kade. You promised me you'd find the man and get me some information before I met him tomorrow. I never left."

Kade moved to the chair nearer to where Talin knelt in front of Lily. "I remember leaving the banquet early. I had a headache. Then, I came here and brought Rylin and Lily over to see our parents before we went to bed. I forget why. But it seemed like a good idea. We didn't stay long. Both of them seemed surprised to see us. We saw you coming down the hall when we left. I got Lily and Rylin here, then went back to find out what you were doing out and about. That's when the explosion happened."

"But you don't remember him showing up at court? Or me talking to you about him after dinner?" Talin asked.

"No. Not really."

"The six of us talked about it in the antechamber, later on. Your mother forbid Lily to even meet him. Told me I couldn't until after she talked with Grayson, found out…"

"Found out if his story checked out. And that you wouldn't meet with him privately until the next day." Rylin broke in, her voice amazed.

Talin whipped his head over her direction. "You remember, then? I'm not crazy and making this up!"

Rylin shook her head slowly, "Everything since we walked into the ceremony seems foggy to me. Almost like I was half asleep."

He turned his attention back to Lily. "Lily, I can prove it to you. All you have to do is use the link. You'll see every single thing I did today." He reached out to her again. Her hand was cold, but she didn't pull away. "Please. Let me prove to you I did not do this," he pleaded with her.

She nodded once, slowly. Talin kept his gaze on her face and opened his mind to her completely. He didn't leave anything guarded.

He felt her presence in his mind, searching. Confusion and pain retreated to relief, then anger as she saw his memories of the past day. Her face softened and she breathed out a heavy sigh. "You didn't do this," she said as she slid out of the chair and embraced him.

"Talin, I hate to interrupt, but we've got a problem." Kade interjected.

"What problem? You all know I didn't do this."

"True, but there were a lot of servants, guards in the hallway before the blast. They won't know. And our parents are injured. There will be some on the Council who'll want you arrested."

"But he's innocent!" Lily cried.

"I know, Lily. He's got to prove it though. Until we find this man, he can't. And I'm willing to bet there's a unit on the way here to arrest you. If you're going to clear your name, we need to get you out of here."

Talin felt Kade's hand grasp the back of his shirt and pull him upward. Following the motion, he stood. "I'm no coward, Kade," he said, facing his friend.

"I'm not saying you are. I'm saying you run now, find who did this. Clear your name before they insist Lily throw you aside to rot."

Lily stood next to him, grabbing his hand. "I'm coming with you."

Kade shook his head. "No, Lily. You have to stay here. With Mom hurt, everyone's going to be looking to you to keep the government moving. You're in charge until she recovers. Rylin will be here to help you. I'll go with Talin, get word to you when we can." The doors to the room rattled. "We have to go now." Stepping around Talin, Kade placed a quick kiss on Rylin's lips.

"I'll cast a shadrim. We don't have time for anything else."

Talin hugged Lily close, whispering "If you need me, just do the link. I'll never close it off to you. Ever." He let her go and moved to the shimmering portal appearing in the center of the room.

The doors crashed open. Talin glanced back at Lily one more time as he stepped into the portal, not knowing where he'd come out.

Chapter Four

Lily crossed her arms under her chest, trying to find a sense of calm. The day had been stressful enough. With the attack, and Talin and Kade both on the run, she felt the last thread of strength she had slowly unraveling.

"Lily," Rylin's voice pulled her from her thoughts. "Grayson's right outside. He wants to come in, says he has to make sure you're all right."

Nodding her assent, Lily swiped at the remaining tears on her face. She didn't turn around though. The spot where the shadrim had been kept her mesmerized. Much as she wanted to use their link, she didn't dare. Not yet. *Kade wouldn't have taken him someplace dangerous,* she reasoned with herself. *They'll be safe. Both of them. And they'll figure this out and Mom and Dad will come out of this perfectly fine and the nightmare will be over.* Her words did little to calm the tide of fear, though.

"Your Royal Highness."

Turning, she faced Grayson. He stood straight, his face expressionless. His uniform was dirty and disheveled A not-so-small group of guardsmen stood behind him.

"How are my parents?"

Grayson bowed, "Being tended to. I'll make sure you get to see them shortly. I've been assured they'll both recover, though it may be some time yet."

"Good. Make sure the small council is convened first thing in the morning. I'll—" she paused, giving herself a moment to make sure the words came out evenly. "I'll address them there, let them know what happened and that I'm prepared to do what must be done until Her Majesty recovers enough to conduct her duties." She finally looked at him. "Before the meeting, though, I expect a full report about the attack. We need to discover who did this, and bring them to Her Majesty for judgement."

Grayson coughed, "Your Highness, we have several witnesses. They claim to have seen Prince Talin, carrying a large parcel just before the explosion. I was told he was in here. Along with Prince Kade." He paused, "If you know where they are now, I need to know. They need to be questioned."

"I have no idea where they are, Grayson." *At least that's not a lie*, she thought. "I can tell you, however, that neither Talin nor Kade had anything to do with this."

"I understand you want to believe that, but…"

"Do you doubt me, Grayson? I share a mental link with Talin. He is my chosen Consort. Kade is my brother. You have known both almost their entire lives, trained them. I have seen Talin's memories of this day. He was not involved." Her voice was louder than she intended, anger at the accusation creeping into her words.

"Aye, I know this. But others do not. I'm leaving some guards both outside and at the door to your bedchamber, Princess. If there was one attack, there may be more." He bowed, then looked at her again. "Be careful, Your Highness. Not everyone will be ready to accept your rule, even temporarily. Especially if they feel Talin is involved." He turned, motioned for some of the guards to stay, and left the room.

The sound of the door shutting behind him made her feel like she was under house arrest.

She looked at Rylin. Her friend shook her head slightly. Rylin was right. Talking over things in front of the guard wouldn't be good. They'd report everything back to Grayson.

"Rylin, please come help me change into something else. I'm hardly dressed to attend my parents in the hospital." Lily moved to the inner door that led to her bedroom. Two of the four guards followed, taking up positions on each side of that door. The others stood at the entry to her suite.

She waited for Rylin to close the door behind them before she threw herself on the bed. Lily didn't even bother to swipe at the tears that ran from her eyes. She was on the edge of losing it, and she knew it. Between the stress of the day, the explosion, Talin and Kade leaving for who knew where….all she wanted to do was scream and throw things.

"What's next, Lily? I know you've got an idea in mind, else you wouldn't have told Grayson to summon the small council." The mattress shifted as Rylin sat down next to her.

She opened her eyes and stared up at the pattern etched into the ceiling tiles. "I at least pretend like I know what I'm doing. I stall. Give Mom time to recover and take a lot of stuff 'under advisement'. And hope that I don't look nearly as terrified as I feel."

"You believe Talin, then?"

Lily sat up. "Yes. I didn't, not at first. I mean, I saw him in the hallway. We all did. But he didn't keep anything from me when I used the link. He was in his room the whole time. He saw this other man, at the end of the ceremony, who said he was his father. I'd give myself a headache trying to figure out why I have holes in my memory of tonight, but I have them. Whoever did this wanted Talin to look guilty, and they almost succeeded." She slid off the bed and grabbed the post with her left hand to steady herself. As she slid her shoes off, she continued, "I mean, it's one thing to disguise yourself in a hallway. But they tried to make everyone forget the man was there to begin with. I may still be a novice with this magic stuff, but that had to have taken a lot to cast a spell of that magnitude. And the cost would've been high." She reached around her back and started to pull at the laces holding the dress tight.

She heard Rylin get off the bed and come up behind her. Her friend pushed her hands away and started to undo the dress. Lily gathered her hair and pulled it over one shoulder. "You said yourself you felt like part of your memory was foggy."

Rylin sighed. "You're probably right, Lily. And anyone that would use that much magic won't be feeling right for at least a day. The cost of the casting aside, it'd exhaust them because they would've had to maintain it for hours. I'm not sure what the purpose of framing Talin would be, though. You're the Successor, not him." The last lace came free and the dress began to slide off of Lily's shoulders.

Stepping out of the dress, she draped it carefully across a chair. "I don't know, but Kade was right. Me knowing the truth won't be enough. They'll have to find the person behind it before his name will truly be cleared." She pulled open a drawer and grabbed a pair of trousers and what passed for a t-shirt. She'd spent weeks trying to convince the tailor that yes, women could wear something this simple. Jeans and a t-shirt were one of the few things she actually missed from her life before Tiadar. She didn't wear them often, but didn't care about appearances now. All she wanted to do was see her parents and help get the rubble cleared so they could assess the damage.

Rylin giggled, "It was one thing to set a new trend with your dress today, Lily. That outfit's going to make some have heart attacks!"

"What's wrong with it?" she demanded. "I'm comfortable. Tonight, that matters more than appearances. I'd rather the staff and kingdom saw me like this, digging in the rubble with everyone else, than on some bloody pedestal. I can move easier, too." She quickly braided her hair, tying it off at the end with a ribbon lying on top of the dresser. "Now, whether Grayson likes it or not, I'm going to go see my parents. You can come with me if you want, or stay here. After that, I'm at least going to see what damage has been done and how fast the clean-up is moving along. Then and only then am I heading to bed." Her face tightened. "I'm used to hard work, Rylin, not sitting down and wringing my hands. I need to do this to keep my mind off of Talin."

Rylin leaned her head to one side, looking Lily up and down. "That actually doesn't look too bad. I might have some made for me." She nodded, "I understand. I'm coming with you. If for no other reason than to give Kade a good story when they come back."

A fresh wave of fear washed over Lily. "They are coming back, right? We don't even know where they went." Tears welled up in her eyes again. All the confidence she built up in herself over the last few minutes threatened to crumble.

Her friend pulled her close and hugged her, "Yes, Lily. They'll both come home. Soon. And they'll bring whoever did this with them," she whispered into her ear.

Lily took a few deep breaths to steady herself once again before stepping back. "Let's do this," she said, and moved to the door.

Two guards stood just outside the door. They looked at her, startled, as she opened the door. Ignoring them, she strode toward the exit from her rooms. Two more guards stood straighter as she approached.

She looked at the two of them and tried to keep her voice from quivering. "We're going to see my parents. I know the way, but understand you may have orders to accompany me. Do that, or stay here. I don't care. But I will get to the hospital one way or another." She put her hand on the latch and opened it.

The door swung outward, scraping small bits of rubble across the floor. She left the room, stopping in the small area outside her rooms.

Torches lit the hallway, illuminating the area for the dozens of people working. Looking up, she saw a gaping hole in the ceiling. The blast was powerful enough to tear open the roof. She knew of a few compounds from the world she grew up in that could do that. Not much here in Tiadar could, though. Whoever planned this had brought the bomb materials from that world. *Shouldn't surprise you, Lily,* she chided herself. *If they went as far as they did, using a shadrim to travel between the worlds and bring back a bomb would be merely part of the plan.*

She stopped someone near her. "Tell the workers up there to be careful. If the blast tore open the roof, the floor could be compromised as well. They need to watch their footing as they clear it."

The woman nodded and moved down the hall, picking her steps carefully.

Lily motioned to Rylin, "Come on. We'll go around. They don't need my help right now."

Cautiously, they moved through the rubble to the junction of hallways nearest her rooms. The door to Talin's rooms was across from her. A guardsman stood at attention, his hand on his rapier and his eyes wary. His rooms were probably being searched now. She turned to the left and jogged to the staircase leading down to what passed as a hospital within Renfel Wood.

Her pace increased as she got closer. She saw the doors at the end of the hall and sprinted, jerking them open.

Several healers moved about in the room. Most were clustered around a pair of beds at the far end. Fear gripped her heart for a moment. She'd been robbed of them without her knowing it for almost fifteen years. Losing them now, six months after Kade found her and brought her home, scared her.

Someone turned and saw her, then turned back to another person. That woman broke away and headed to Lily.

"Your Royal Highness," she said as she approached. "You are not hurt?"

Lily stopped but kept her gaze focused on the two beds. She couldn't see who was on them. "No, we're fine. My parents?" Her voice cracked slightly.

"Their Majesties were injured, but not beyond our ability to heal. The medications we gave them, however, will take time to work. They're out of danger, but it may be several days before they recover."

"I want to see them. Please." She prayed that it didn't come across like an order, but she was ready to give one if she had to.

"Of course." The woman moved aside and fell into step beside Lily.

The others parted around her father first. Corvin lay on a bed, his eyes closed. Blood seeped from a wound on the side of his face. The steady rise and fall of his chest relieved her. She moved next to him, taking one of his hands into hers. For a moment, she remembered something Erena had told her growing up. That men had 'big hands to beat girls who didn't obey them'. Her father had proven that false, more than once. He'd never raised a hand against her in anger, and had been nothing but loving and patient in the months since she'd come back to Tiadar.

"Hey, why the tears? I don't look that bad, do I?" Corvin's voice was low, tired. He kept his eyes shut.

Lily swiped gently at the drops of water on his arm. "A bit worse for wear, but not terrible," she replied.

"Was anyone killed?" he asked.

"Not that I know of. Mom's here—they're taking care of her as well. The healers say you'll both be fine in a few days."

"Good to hear. Kade?"

"Kade's fine." She tried to keep her voice light.

Corvin opened his eyes slightly and looked at her. "He left, didn't he? With Talin?"

Lily nodded, "Talin didn't do this, Dad. He had me link up with him, see his memories. This wasn't him."

His eyes closed again, muttering something Lily couldn't make out. She waited a moment, watching him sleep, before gently placing his hand back on the bed.

Wiping at the tears, she moved over to the other bed. Keryth was awake. A healer worked on her ankle, wrapping a bandage tight around it. Lily waited out of the way near the bed for the man to finish.

Keryth met her gaze, wincing as the healer finished his work and moved her foot back under the blankets. "Thank you," she said. "Please, go work on someone else. Let me talk with my daughter privately." Everyone left the area in a hurry, giving them space.

"It wasn't Talin," Lily began.

Keryth raised a bandaged hand and she stopped. "I want to believe that, Lily. We raised him after his mother died, after all. And you chose him as your Consort. But we raised Iris, too."

Lily moved closer to the head of the bed. She grabbed a wooden stool nearby and pulled it closer as she sat down. "He had me use the link, let me see every memory he had of tonight. There was someone else. Someone that none of us remembered seeing at first."

Keryth narrowed her eyes at Lily's words. "Someone else?"

"He had a memory of a man coming at the end of the ceremony. He claimed to be Talin's father. You had him taken off to get ready for the feast. Told Talin he wasn't supposed to go near him until you could verify his identity. Talin saw him at dinner, but then he disappeared. It wasn't until he brought him up that Kade or Rylin remembered him. Rylin," Lily gestured to where her friend stood at the far end of the room, "said she felt like her memories of the night were foggy."

"Do you remember seeing him?"

"No, not currently. But I have a hard time believing those three don't and they're making this up."

Keryth leaned back on the pillows, "And I take it you and Rylin let Kade and Talin run off to get evidence to clear his name?"

Lily looked away from her, "Well…" she hesitated.

"Never mind. You just answered my question. I'm not saying it was wrong of them to do so," Keryth chided her, "but I would've wanted to speak with them first."

"The healers say you'll both be here for several days. I told Grayson to convene the small council in the morning. I'll at least give them an update on the two of you, make sure things stay on track."

"Good. Don't let some of them bully you into doing anything, Lily. While the small council generally is friendly, there's still some opportunists in there. I recommend against signing anything. It could be Talin's death warrant." She slouched down a bit more. "They must've spiked my tea already," she said, her voice sleepy. "I trust you, Lily, to do what has to be done. Remember. It's not always about what we want to do but what we have to do." Her voice trailed off as her eyes closed.

Lily stood and kissed her mother on her forehead. "I'll remember," she whispered.

Chapter Five

A blast of cold air hit Talin as he emerged from the shadrim. Shivering, he briskly rubbed his hands up and down his arms in an attempt to warm them. "Where the hell are we?" he asked, his teeth chattering.

Kade pointed to a dark corner of the unlit room. "There's coats in there, and some packs. Grab one. We have to move fast before the caretaker realizes we were here."

Talin headed to the wardrobe and pulled open the doors. Heavy parkas, lined with fur, hung from hooks. Gloves sat on a shelf above the coats, while two packs sat on the floor. "Talk to me, Kade," he demanded as he grabbed one of the garments and started to put it on.

His friend walked over and mimicked his movements. "Not here," he kept his voice low. "I promise you, I'll give you answers. But we're far from having you anyplace safe yet."

Talin shoved his arms into the coat, anger and frustration warring in him for supremacy. Kade had never kept a secret from him, not like this. Sure, once or twice when there were too many people around. But this room was deserted. As far as he could tell, the entire house was. His hands worked at the closures as he glared at Kade. "I'm not a child, Kade. You and I don't keep secrets. But you can't even tell me where--"

Kade's dark head snapped up and he held up a hand. "You're going to have to trust me on this, Talin. Once we're out of the house, when it's safe to talk, we will. But the caretaker here is honor bound to report to the Queen the presence of *any* unscheduled arrivals. And that report's normally given in the presence of the small council. If we're going to keep you safe, we have to leave." Talin took the pack Kade shoved at him. "Now."

Nodding, Talin shut up. He still wasn't thrilled. Not by a long shot. But everything that'd happened over the last few hours was insane. The only way he'd clear his name, be able to go back and face Lily, was to prove his innocence. Having the small council find out his whereabouts wasn't going to help.

Kade had shut the doors. He pushed against the wardrobe, and it slid silently aside. The outline of a door, faint in the early dawn light filtering into the room, sat in the wall. Talin watched, his eyes wide, as Kade ran his fingers over one section of the wall. "I always forget where the latch is," he muttered. "Aha," he said as the panel slid to one side. The other side was a gaping black hole.

"Go ahead," Kade said, motioning Talin forward. "I've got to close it behind us. Don't wander too far, though. I'll get us some light when the door's sealed again."

Talin shouldered his pack and walked into the inky darkness.

Once he passed the threshold, he reached out with both hands trying to find a wall. He found it quickly. The passage was narrow—they wouldn't be able to walk side by side. The walls were smoothed stone. One solid piece from what he could tell. No seams or grout to make him think it was built by men.

The slight sound of wood against wood made him turn his head back. Kade was sliding the wardrobe back into place, using a pair of handles protruding slightly from the rear of the cabinet. A clicking noise echoed slightly in the tunnel as the door slid back into place. Leaving them standing in a darkness so complete, Talin wasn't able to see his own gloved hand as he waved it in front of his face.

"Just a second," Kade said. Talin heard him rummaging about. A spark glowed for a moment, then grew as it caught the wick of a candle. Kade knelt on the floor, a lantern in front of him. "It's not much, I know,"

Kade told Talin as he placed the candle into the lantern and shut the door. "But it'll keep us from tripping over our own feet until we get to where we're going."

"Where, exactly, is that?" Talin asked as he watched his friend rise and adjust his pack.

Kade picked up the lantern and moved closer to Talin. "We're in a small home, built on the side of Elivin Mountains." Talin jumped at the name. "The other side, Talin. We're not near Racne's house. Besides, even if we were, it belongs to the Crown now. That was one of the things Heren had to give up in order to spare his life. Mom stripped him of his titles and plans to have the building razed to the ground."

Talin pressed himself as flat against the wall as he could as his friend moved past him. "There's an area back in the mountain itself where we can rest. Talk. It has a water source. I promise, Talin, you can ask any question you want to when we reach it. And I will answer them. But we're still too close to being found right now." Kade turned around and started to walk down the tunnel.

Talin took a deep breath and started to follow the meager light in Kade's hand. For some reason, he began to wonder if the answers were ones he wanted to hear.

Yes, Racne had spun her web in a keep nestled at the foot of this mountain range. Conjured up creatures best left alone to do her bidding. Rylin had been directly affected by some of that magic. Racne'd even tried to make her Maiten as a means to keep Lily in line. He was glad the healers had been able to remove the brand on Rylin. Kade stayed by her side as the procedure happened, giving the woman he loved his support. Talin had watched from outside the room, glad he didn't have to hear the screams.

The thing was, there were rumors of other creatures that called these peaks home. Some so fearful or fantastical that stories of their existence were used by parents to scare their children into behaving. As the weight of the mountain surrounded him, he started to think the stories might have some truth to them.

For who else would live in the dark but monsters?

The terrain was smooth, well worn. "Kade," Talin asked, "who built this trail?"

"I don't know," he answered, keeping his head forward. "It's been here for as long as the Fomori have been on Tiadar, though."

They walked in silence. Something about the weight of the rock around him made Talin nervous. He lost track of time. *At least there's no other tunnels*, he thought, *I can make it back if I have to.*

Kade led them around a bend and Talin's heart sank. The large cavern before them had at least six different tunnels leading off of it that he could see in the meager light of the candle. There'd be no way he'd remember what one they'd come from.

"This is where we'll rest," Kade said, his voice echoing slightly. He moved to a tunnel to the right. "Most of these are waystations of a sort. Small antechambers for travelers to rest undisturbed."

"What would disturb us here, Kade? We're deep in a mountain," Talin commented as he followed his friend.

"It's not for our safety, Talin. There are…residents in this mountain. Come inside. It's better if we stay out of sight as much as possible."

Talin crouched down to avoid hitting his head and made his way down the passage. He heard a trickle of water coming from ahead. It grew warmer, too. Warm enough that his hands began to sweat in the thick gloves. Just as his legs began to protest, the tunnel ended in a good-sized room tall enough for him to stand up in.

Kade was at a table, lighting some candles. The gentle glow began to reflect off of crystals embedded in the walls, illuminating the room. Two cots sat off to one side. Water fell gently from a crevice in the opposite wall, pooling slightly before draining down a smaller crack and back into the mountain. Shrugging off his pack, he dropped it on the floor. "What is this place?" he asked.

"I told you. It's a waystation. The ones who live in the mountain found it better to provide travelers places like this to rest over having them find—" Kade hesitated "—other places to try and stay."

Talin pulled off the gloves and set them on the table before working the clasps on his coat. "These people don't sound like they like strangers, Kade. How can you be certain we're safe here?"

"There's a treaty." To Talin's ear, there was a wealth of missing information that Kade didn't say in those three words.

Talin pulled a chair out from the table and sat down. Resting his forearms on the table, he studied his oldest friend. His movements were jerky; he moved too fast. He was nervous.

And he wouldn't look at Talin.

"Kade, you promised me answers when we got someplace safe. I'm guessing this is the spot. I played by your rules. Now, talk to me. What is this place really? And who are we avoiding?"

Talin watched as Kade slumped in a chair, a defeated air about him. The tension grew as Kade rubbed his hands on his face, then absently traced a non-existent line on the table in front of him.

"This mountain is home to the Tuatha De Danaan that fled Eire when the Fomori did."

Talin started, shocked at Kade's words. "That's impossible, Kade. We fled them as they came after us, bent on slaughtering every single Fomorian they could find. There's no way they would've been allowed to follow us here."

"I didn't want to believe it either, Talin, when Dad first told me. The house we were at is built into the mountain. Remember how Dad and I would disappear for a few hours after the Longest Night celebrations were over? We came here, to meet with them. Renew the treaty. This is the job of the Consort. When Lily had been gone for ten years, I started coming with him. In case she didn't return and take a Consort before he died."

Staring at the wall, Talin tried to digest what Kade told him. He raised his head and looked at his friend. "What's in this treaty?" he asked. "And how did this happen in the first place?"

Kade let out a deep breath. "The Tuatha De had been slaughtering us for years, especially the ones that were strong with magic. The handful of Fomori who were still strong enough to cast a shadrim the size that would be needed were going to die in the casting. One of the Tuatha De approached them, a woman named Kronos. She promised aid in the casting as long as we brought a handful of families with us. They claimed they didn't like the politics and hatred their race was practicing. Aeowolf was King, Cerridwen his Consort. She negotiated with Kronos and the rest who wanted to come with us. Got them to agree to stay hidden here in the mountain. We would give them a home, within reason.

"The treaty guarantees that they'll stay apart from the Fomori, not make themselves known to the rest of Tiadar. They know we'd slaughter them if they ever came out of the mountain. The hatred still runs deep. We come, once a year, to shake hands and stay at peace. The original pact states that each group can ask a single favor of the other every five years. It's not something done lightly. Dad considered enlisting their aid to find Lily, but Mom was steadfast against it. In all the years I've come here, I've never heard him ask for a single thing from them other than to remain hidden per the original promise."

"But now you want to ask for their help to exonerate me?" Talin barely got the words out.

Kade nodded, finally turning his head to face Talin. “They’re not monsters, Talin. Not the ones that have met with Dad and me, anyway. And their magic works differently than ours.”

“Why would they do this, though?” Skepticism tinted his words. “I don’t know, Kade. There’s got to be a better way to put the pieces together. We just have to find Iris. It wouldn’t surprise me at all if she was behind this.”

“How do you plan to do that, Talin? We have no leads other than ones that point right at you. The magic used to block our memories of the stranger is elvish magic. Danaan magic. They’re capable of making you forget years have gone by. If one of their own has left the mountain, the treaty’s been broken. They will want to catch that person faster than we do, see them held accountable. One of them going out into Tiadar is a threat to them all.”

“You should listen, Consort. Your adviser is wise beyond his years.”

Talin jerked his head toward the sound of the voice. Standing in the doorway was a woman. Three others moved into the room behind her. Each had pale skin and hair, and bright blue eyes.

And they were armed.

“The Tuatha De Danaan welcome the Consort to their realm,” the woman intoned, bowing to Talin. “You are both invited to the Stronghold, to take counsel with the King on how to resolve this conflict.”

Talin exchanged a glance with Kade, then looked back at the newcomers. “We’re, um, honored. Truly. But we’ve traveled far enough for one day.”

The woman smiled, cold and humorless. “One does not refuse our King, Consort. I recommend you rethink your refusal.”

“And if I don’t?”

The three other warriors stepped aside, allowing more into the room. A dozen or more moved about the room, drawing their weapons. “Then we’ll have to insist,” she said. The last word came out as a hiss, emphasized by the sound of her weapon leaving its’ sheath.

Talin stood. He and Kade had few weapons on them. They wouldn’t stand a chance in a fight, not this time.

Chapter Six

He couldn't make out how they did it, but the Danaans possessed something that made the path through the caverns easier to see. The light was dim, muted, but did the job. No smoke, and it didn't flicker. Talin admitted to himself that he was more than a bit curious over what it was.

He was also hopelessly lost. Their guide had taken so many twist and turns, he knew he'd never find his way back out without one of them to guide him.

"I don't suppose you came down this far with your father?" he whispered to Kade.

His friend shook his head, and pressed a finger to his lips.

The leader snapped her head around, glaring at him. He clenched his jaw, but kept silent. *Fine*, he thought, *we're not supposed to talk. They're treating us more like prisoners than guests. Yet I'm supposed to trust them. This isn't helping.*

His mind wandered to Lily. *I don't know if you can hear me,* he sent out, *but I hope things are okay there. That your parents are recovering well, and the burden you took up isn't yours for long. I'll come back to you. I promise.*

A wave of emotions crashed over him. Love, anxiety, and confusion hit all at once. She didn't answer him with words, but he knew she heard him. That the connection with her still worked this far away from each other gave him comfort. Rylin was with her, too. She could steady Lily in ways Talin hadn't figured out yet.

The glow that surrounded them gained in strength. Their guide stopped and turned to them. The mouth of the tunnel opened up behind her, illuminating her. She spoke for the first time since they left the waystation. "It is not often we welcome Fomori to the Stronghold. I recommend you do not wander off without an escort." She stepped aside and motioned Talin and Kade to move past her.

Talin glanced at Kade as they stepped forward. His friend's face was calm, unemotional. The face of someone who'd spent a lifetime in the public eye. He knew Kade's tells, though. The slight twitch in the corner of his left eye let Talin know Kade was just as cautious about what was ahead as he was.

The tunnel opened onto a large platform. Stairs led down from each side. The mountain itself had been gutted. Instead of dirt and stone, a city that rivaled Renfel Keep in size sat in the cavernous opening. Across from the ledge they stood on, above all else, sat a castle carved from crystal so clear it could've been ice. Two pillars flanked the structure. Molten rock churned within the columns, alternating between bright red and deepest black. The entire city was bathed in a deep red glow.

"Come," their guide spoke again. "The King of the Elves does not wait patiently."

Talin looked at Kade, waiting for him to follow their escort. "You're the Consort," he said. "You get to go first." The corners of Kade's mouth twitched with amusement as Talin started. He still was getting used to outranking Kade.

"Are we permitted to speak or ask questions now?" Talin asked as they made their way down one of the staircases.

"You can ask. I may not answer," she replied.

"Fair enough. What's the name of the city?"

She kept moving. Talin watched his feet closely. The steps were wide, but unfamiliar. And there was no rail on one side. Someone who wasn't cautious could easily fall to their death.

"Technically, we call it Eire. The Stronghold is the residence of the royal family. As this is the only place we are *permitted* to live, most simply call it home."

Talin heard a bitterness in the way she said the one word. He'd spent too much time around the royal family growing up not to learn some statecraft. The inflection was enough to tell him that the original treaty might well be in danger. As he was the Consort, he'd be the one to renegotiate any terms. At least, that's how Kade described everything. The Consort had allowed the Danaans to come with them to Tiadar, and the Consort met with them each year. *Don't make any promises*, he told himself. *The Queen and Lily need to make the decision. You only have to deliver the message.*

"Do you have a name?"

"Yes. I am called Chadine."

"And your King? What is his name?"

"He will tell you what he wants you to call him." Chadine's tone was brisk, short.

Talin shut up.

They reached the first level of the city and walked past an assortment of buildings. Some were built into the wall of the cavern, while others were freestanding. Looking around, he could see more tunnels hiding behind.

Posts stood at corners. Each one radiated a muted light, illuminating the area enough to see where they were going. "What powers the lights?" he asked, his curiosity finally getting the better of him.

"The mountain does." Chadine pointed at the red and black columns on each side of the Stronghold. "The heat from the core is great. Our ancestors harnessed it, taught others how to maintain the system. They are able to control it so we know when it is daytime in the world above and when it is night. This is brighter than normal, but your eyes have not yet adjusted to our world. You will see this yourselves, when you retire for the night, how dark our lives have become."

Talin looked around, trying to gauge the brightness of the cavern to what time it would be. He and Kade had left Renfel Keep shortly after midnight. They'd walked for a few hours before reaching the waystation. Then, the march here. It had to be close to midafternoon, or a little later. He hoped they weren't here so long that he'd get used to the fake sunlight.

There were elves moving about. Men, women, and children. Not a lot, but some. Many stopped to stare at them. The faces were mostly curious, but a few were openly hostile. The majority of the populace was a sea of pale hair and blue eyes. They appeared well fed and happy. Occasionally, he'd see someone sitting in a doorway with red or brown hair. In contrast, they were unkempt, dirty. They wouldn't look up as they passed but kept their heads down. One, a young child, dared to raise her head. Her eyes were dark orbs in hollow sockets. She was starving to death. The child pushed a frail hand through her hair. For a moment, Talin caught a glimpse of her ear. Instead of the slender point, it looked mangled. As if the singular physical feature marking her as Danaan had been cut away.

"Why are there children starving in the streets?" he asked, uncomprehending. That was something he always respected about Keryth. Poverty had been eradicated. It became law to welcome in someone who was in need, unless the Crown dictated otherwise.

Chadine snorted, her voice full of distaste. "We are the Tuatha De Danaan. We care for our own, not the castoffs of your making."

Talin stopped talking again. Inwardly, he seethed. He'd never heard of anyone in Tiadar throwing out a child. His mother told him of how she brought him to Court, asking for work. And how Keryth had given her a job within the palace, and a room for both of them. They weren't shunned, but welcomed.

Talin looked back at the child again. Her dark hair fell in greasy, tangled strands down her back. If not for the ears, she could be Fomorian.

He scanned the area again. Kade said only a few families had come here during the exodus from Eire. Even given the centuries that had passed since then, there were more Danaan than there should've been. There'd always been stories of travelers being lost in these mountains, never to be seen again. Talin started to wonder if they'd found their way here. Or had been led.

They were led up the wide steps leading to the Stronghold. No guards stood outside the doors. "Your lives must be peaceful ones," Kade remarked, "if your King can remain unguarded."

Chadine spun, her face tight with anger. "Our lives are the best we can make, living as we do. Our King fears nothing. Not even your kind." She turned back around and strode purposefully up the steps.

Talin exchanged a glance with Kade. Whatever the treaty stated, it clearly wasn't something every Danaan thought was good.

A single thought entered Talin's head as they walked through the massive crystal doors. He'd somehow left one dangerous situation and gotten himself into something much more deadly.

Inside, the polished stone walls and floor gleamed. The sound of their footsteps echoed throughout the entry as their escort led them to a pair of ornate doors at the other end.

As they approached, the doors parted. The chamber ahead wasn't large, but it was built to impress. Elaborately carved columns stood at precise intervals along the sides. The stone floor was carpeted down the center with a vibrant red. At the end, sitting on a raised dais, sat two ornate thrones. The light bounced off them, producing an abundance of color. On one throne sat a man. His timeless face was impassive. The crown that rested on his brow seemed to constantly move and shift.

"Be careful, Talin." Kade spoke under his breath, barely loud enough for Talin to hear.

Talin shot his friend a look of concern. Kade kept his eyes on the King. "That's not who reigned last year."

Talin cringed. A new reign usually meant new policies. And new treaties. He was going to have to tread carefully if they were going to get out of here.

The man rose as they approached. Chadine bowed and moved to one side. "All hail Fuil, King of the Tuatha De Danaan! Ruler of Eire."

"Welcome, Consort. It is a pleasure to meet you. Your future brother-in-law accompanies you. I hope that does not bode ill for Corvin?" The man's voice was smooth, pleasant.

"No, Corvin yet lives. As does Keryth." Talin replied. "There was, however, an attempt on their lives. That's why we've come to you. We're trying to find the people behind it."

Fuil started, but recovered quickly. "Ah, I see. I had not heard. We rarely get news of what happens on the surface. I am…" Fuil hesitated for just a moment, but Talin caught it. "Pleased that Keryth and Corvin's reign will continue for many years to come." He clapped his hands together, rubbing them briskly. "I hate to make this short, but matters of state need my attention. I'm sure you understand. If you'd follow Anstara," he gestured to a woman who hovered near the end of the dais, "she'll see you to suitable quarters. Tonight, the three of us will chat over dinner. We can discuss more then."

Talin bowed slightly, understanding their audience was at an end. He fell into step next to Kade. Glancing back, he saw Fuil deep in conversation with Chadine. No doubt reporting everything they said or did on the trek here. It would be the first thing he would want to know if he and Lily sat on the throne, that's for certain. And it would give Fuil the advantage.

The walk was brief, down a side corridor leading from the main hall. They passed less than a dozen Danaans, all of which openly stared at them. Some with hatred and contempt plainly visible on their faces.

Their guide stopped in front of a plain wood door. "You can rest here. His Majesty will send for you when the night meal is prepared." She turned the handle and pulled the door open before waving them in.

The room was beyond ornate. Gold and silver was inlaid among stone and wood furniture. Polished gemstones served as drawer handles. Two small beds sat off to one side.

A soft click reached Talin's ear. Turning, he saw the door had been closed. He took a few steps toward it, intent on trying the latch.

"I wouldn't bother, Talin. They locked us in here." Kade's voice was tired.

"Are we guests or prisoners, then?" Talin asked, one hand passing across the smooth top of a small table as he went back to the center of the room.

Kade slouched in a chair, his legs reaching out in front of him. "I don't know, but I fear we're the latter."

Talin sank into a seat across from his friend. "Talk to me, Kade. You know what we're dealing with. I didn't even know these—" he hesitated "—people existed until this morning. You've been talking to them for a couple years. But I'm the bloody Consort, so I gotta do the talking now. And I can't do that if I don't know details." Try as he might, he couldn't keep the anger out of his voice.

"Calm down, Talin. It's not like you weren't going to be told about this. I know Dad would've sat down with you, got you up to speed before he had to make the trek again. Everything was rather unexpected."

"Calm down? I have someone framing me for attempted murder! I trusted you to help me figure this out, get me someplace safe, and end up in a castle surrounded by *elves*!" He thrust a hand toward the door, "They're the reason we had to leave Eire in the first place! And you want me to trust them enough to ask for their help?" He knew he was shouting but didn't care. The walls were stone, probably too thick for anyone to hear him. At least, that's what he told himself.

Rage and frustration boiled inside him. Unable to sit still, he jumped out of the chair and started to pace. "You said each party can ask for a favor every five years, right? Have they ever asked anything of you or Corvin?"

"Not when I was present, no. Though Dad mentioned once, in passing, that a favor was asked of him and he granted it. What it was, I don't know."

Talin stopped, his hands pushed against the stone wall. He could feel the warmth that ran behind the stone. Begrudgingly, he admitted to himself that he wished they could copy the design if only to keep things warm during a harsh winter. "Well, it's not like I can ask them to go back to Eire. They don't have a home beyond this mountain to go back to."

He heard Kade turn in his chair, felt his eyes on him. "What do you mean? Lily lived on Earth, where Eire was. The land still exists. She told me they called it Ireland or something like that."

Pushing away from the wall, he looked at his friend. "Remember when I stayed there for a while, got a job at Lily's school? Because I thought for sure she was there? I learned a few things. Even sat down and read some of their history books. The Tuatha were chased out of Eire by a race called either Milesians or Celts. Who were then overrun by a religious sect, the Christians. Any more, the idea of elves are considered myths. Stuff of legend and folklore." He pointed at the door again, "If Fuil walked out of a shadrim and back onto Eire, they'd think he was insane. The world Lily left is messed up, Kade. There's nothing but hatred and war." He snorted, "Maybe they'd fit right in after all. That's all they were before they came here. Think they'd move back if I asked them to?"

Kade's eyes narrowed. "I can tell you this much. There's not a single thing His Majesty agreed to that Her Majesty did not know about. Nor did His Majesty ever attempt to negotiate new terms without consulting her."

Throwing his arms up in frustration, Talin gave up. "I get it. I'm not just me anymore, but an extension of Lily's rule." He leaned heavily against the wall, sliding down to sit on the floor.

"You're the Consort, Talin. You agreed to fill that role for Lily. Which means you can't do anything here that you think she'd disapprove of. Or that Queen Keryth would."

Talin ran a weary hand through his hair. "I know, Kade. It's just…I feel like we're chickens and the foxes have us surrounded."

"Can you talk to Lily, let her know where we are?"

He shook his head. "No. I don't know why, but the most I can get is perceptions, ideas of what she's feeling. It's like we're too far away or there's too much of something between us. Even if I could, how would I possibly be able to explain this to her right now? She grew up hearing that elves were a myth." He laughed. "Come to think of it, the same history book said Fomorians crawled back into a bog. That's how her world saw our exodus. We drowned ourselves in muck."

Exhaustion started to overwhelm him. Talin looked at the two beds. "Fuil said we'd meet him for dinner. I don't know about you, but I've had a long day. Coronation, the banquet, the attack, all of it. I'm going to take advantage of getting some sleep while I can. Something tells me we're going to need it." He pushed himself off the floor and moved toward the closest bed. The mattress cradled his form as he collapsed on the top. He didn't hear Kade's reply.

Chapter Seven

"The queen that was before Fuil, her name was Kronos? But you said that was the leader of the Tuatha when they came through with the rest of us?" Talin asked, confused.

"It was the same woman, I'm certain of it. The Tuatha live even longer than we do. Dad once joked that Kronos would be dealing with us for another six reigns." Kade dipped his hands into a bowl of water that sat on top of a dresser. Splashing the contents on his face, he rubbed his hands across his face before reaching for a towel. "I never met Fuil. It was always Kronos and one or two others that came to the waystation to meet us. She mentioned she had sons, though."

Talin leaned against a wall. "What's the likelihood that Fuil had a hand in his mother's death?"

"That is something I won't speculate on," Kade tossed the towel back on the counter. "I don't trust him, though. He seems friendly and all, but his messenger was colder than a glacier."

"Yeah. Chadine certainly wasn't happy about her mission." Talin paused. "How'd they even know we were there? I mean, they came right there. We weren't even in the cave for ten minutes."

"Dad long suspected there was an alarm of some sort in the mountain. Or that the Tuatha watched the tunnels in some way. We never stayed in that room long once we got there before they showed up. He wasn't too concerned. Said it was nice to know that anyone who stumbled on the tunnels by accident would be redirected back out. An integral part of the treaty is that they stay separate from us."

"Kade, you and I both know that didn't happen. You saw the same thing I did as we came through the city.

There was ample evidence that they've not only met with Formorians, but had children. And those children aren't being well treated." The sight of the small girl with the mangled ear refused to leave his memory.

Before Kade could respond, the sound of a key in the door alerted them that someone was coming. Talin shot a look at his friend. Ready or not, dinner with their host was about to begin.

Anstara walked into the room, her hands folded in front of her. "His Majesty invites you to dine with him. If you would follow me, I am to lead you to him." Pausing, she glanced at the rapiers hanging from their belts. "It is not wise to go before the King of the Tuatha so armed."

Talin drew his weapon and laid it on the bed. Kade followed suit.

She held one arm toward the door, inviting them to leave.

Talin waited until he was closer to her. "Could we have a tour of the keep on our way?" he asked.

The pale blue eyes hardened. "It is unwise, Consort, to go exploring. Few of our kind have fond memories of your race." Her voice was stern.

Nodding his understanding, Talin kept from asking any other questions. *Fond memories indeed*, he thought. *They're the reason we had to leave Eire! We didn't commit genocide—they did!*

The hallway was deserted outside of the three of them and an armed escort. Not even a maid carrying a tray. "Does everyone eat at the same time here?" Kade asked. To Talin, his voice sounded overly cheery.

"His Majesty felt it wiser if you were not seen more than was necessary. While we all know of the treaty, many here remember the exodus. He was concerned that some may become…*agitated*…at the sight of a Fomorian in the Stronghold." Her step quickened.

The knot in Talin's stomach tightened. For the first time in hours, he was glad his connection with Lily was so weak. The last thing he needed was for her to know how afraid he was.

He'd at least admit that to himself. This went beyond any battle he'd been in. Not that there'd been many of them. Keryth had led Tiadar into a time of peace. Still, there were always Houses that thought about breaking away. They were just more blatant about it than Heren and Jasper had been. Suddenly, it hit him. The game of politics was a far more dangerous battlefield than one with swords or spears. And he really didn't have a clue how to beat someone at the game.

They stopped at a nondescript door. "His Majesty awaits you inside," Anstara announced.

Exchanging a quick glance with Kade, Talin replied, "Thank you," and reached out to turn the handle.

It swung inward on silent hinges, and they stepped inside.

The room was richly furnished. A table with room for six sat in the center. The dark wood frame gleamed from a hidden light source. Color exploded across the crystal top. Their host stood at the head, a place on each side for them.

"Welcome, Consort. You and the Prince are most welcome at my table." The friendliness of his tone sounded forced.

Talin bowed, "We're grateful for the chance to, um…" His mind refused to work. "Well, I know there's some courtly language I should be using but it escapes me right now." Laughing, he continued, "Kade and I are both grateful for your hospitality, however."

Fuil smiled and waved a hand toward the extra seats. "Come, sit. We'll eat. We can dispose of all the formalities if that makes you more comfortable. After all, I understand you're fairly new to the role you now have."

Moving around the table, Talin put a hand on the back of one of the chairs. "Thank you. I've been part of the royal household for as long as I can remember." He took a seat. "But it's a bit different when you're part of the guard versus Consort."

Fuil sat as well. "Ah, yes. I remember hearing you'd been a soldier before this all happened. To be honest, the courtly graces can be trying, at times. It's refreshing to be able to sit and converse with someone without having to worry about titles and the like." He turned to Kade. "What do you think, Your Highness? Shall we drop the pretense or does that offend you?"

Kade smiled, and Talin instantly knew he was on his guard. "By all means, we should be comfortable. Talin will be meeting you every year to renew the treaty, after all. There's no reason to not be pleasant about it." His voice was calm.

"Of course, there is the treaty. And we will discuss that. At length. But, after we eat." Fuil rang a small bell and servants came in with domed trays. "It's not often we have guests here at the Stronghold," he continued, "so I fear the cook went overboard. I hope you're both hungry."

A dish was placed before Talin and the lid removed. Meat, gravy, and a few things Talin couldn't identify filled the plate before him. A quick glance showed that Fuil and Kade had the same meal in front of them. He picked up a fork and pushed aside what looked like a vegetable. Something else resembling a centipede lay dead underneath it. His stomach rebelled against the thought. *Just eat*, he chided himself. *Don't think about it.*

About halfway through the meal, Fuil spoke, "I'm sorry to hear about the attempt on Keryth's life," he said between mouthfuls. "Do you know who might have been behind it?"

Talin shot a look at Kade. He knew he was the one to answer, but how much to tell them was another story.

"Someone showed up at the Coronation ceremony that wasn't expected. It's our thought that this man was behind it. Or he'd know who was. He disappeared. We were going to try and locate him when we were invited here."

"Interesting. Who was this person?" Fuil's gaze rested on Talin.

"He said he was my father."

Fuil's body jerked. He dabbed at the corners of his mouth with a napkin. "That's impossible. Your father's buried here in Eire, Consort. He died before you were born."

Talin's mind reeled from the news. "Why would my father be buried here? He was Fomori, not Danaan."

"Come," Fuil rose, "I'll take you to his grave. We'll talk on the way."

Talin and Kade stood and followed Fuil out the door. The King waved his guard to stand down. "It's not far, and is sacred ground. None would harm me there." He spoke as they went down a corridor to a narrow door. "The crypt is down here." He placed the palm of his hand against the wall and the rock began to glow, illuminating a spiral staircase cut out of the rock. "It can get steep, so I recommend you use the rail," he cautioned.

"Your mother came to us in a daze. She'd been thrown out of her village for some reason. I can't say I remember the exact reason. I don't know why my mother took pity on her, but she did that from time to time. Let a Fomori join our realm. It rarely ended well." He moved quickly, making it hard for Talin to keep up. "Your father fell in love with her, despite his family's wishes. When he died, they wanted nothing to do with her. Not even when they found out she was with child. They put a lot of pressure on Mother, demanding she be killed before you could be born. She had a soft spot in her heart for her, though, and refused to let them slaughter her."

They rounded one more curve and came to a stop. The cavern before them opened up farther than Talin could see. Set into crystal columns by the hundreds were bodies.

"He's over here," Fuil called.

Talin walked slowly over to the cluster of crystals the Danaan stood next to. The face of the man he'd seen at Coronation rested inside one of the spires.

"My mother decided to do the unthinkable," Fuil said. "She asked Corvin for a boon as per the treaty. She asked him to take your mother out of here. Let the two of you live." Bitterness and hatred tainted his words. "Her weakness toward my brother and his 'wife' was his undoing. Letting her first grandchild be a mongrel was beyond treason. The Tuatha De Danaan are a noble race, and you Fomori rats are all that stand between us and the surface."

Talin spun, his hand instinctually going to where his rapier should be. The fear he'd felt solidified at Fuil's words.

Several dozen armed Danaans surged from behind the columns, surrounding them. He looked at Fuil. "Whatever you think to gain by killing us, it won't happen."

"Kill you? No, not yet." He snapped his fingers and the soldiers rushed in to restrain both of them.

Talin dodged the first two, only to be rewarded with a kick to the groin. He heard Kade fighting as more jumped on him. His arms were restrained and they forced him to stand next to Kade. His friend had blood trickling from his forehead.

"You, Consort," Fuil spat at Talin, "will remain here. I need to get to know my nephew, after all." He turned to Kade. "You will go back and deliver a message to Keryth. Tell her the Tuatha De Danaan no longer agree to stay hidden away. She will come here, agree to a new treaty, or else we will unleash our might upon the surface.

When we are done, there will be no Fomori left for her to rule. She will come, or she will die."

"And Talin's your hostage to ensure she'll come? I know my mother's will. She does not make deals with terrorists." Kade's face was red with anger as he struggled against the hands that held him.

Fuil moved up to them, his body inches away from the two of them. Talin's heart beat rapidly as adrenalin surged through his body. His mind reeled with the thought that his father was Danaan.

"If she does not, I'll take the Consort out of this mountain. Where the link he shares with Keryth's beloved daughter is strong. And then I will break his body. I will torture his soul. I will make her feel every single bit of pain I inflict on him. When she's writhing on the ground, weeping for his fate, Keryth will come. If that doesn't work, I'll start to send Lily pieces of him. I will drive the Successor mad until Keryth comes. This I promise to you." He jerked his head once and the guards began to drag Kade away.

Talin twisted his body, hoping to jar one or more of his captors loose. Pain flared across the back of his knees as the blow hit. His legs buckled and he fell to the floor.

Fuil's legs blocked his vision. Talin gritted his teeth as they pulled his hair, forcing him to look up. The king's face was twisted as he stared down at him. All Talin could do was watch the fist as it headed toward his jaw.

Chapter Eight

Kade winced as the rope cut into his wrists, but he kept trying to find some way to loosen the knots. His escort had dropped off from the number that initially pulled him from the crystal graveyard. There were only four leading him to the surface. At least, he hoped that's where they were taking him.

The darkness was absolute. Even if he could get his hands free, he wouldn't know if he was swinging at a face or a wall. The last thing he saw was Fuil's fist making contact with Talin's jaw, pushing him to the ground.

He's unconscious, that's all, Kade told himself. *Fuil needs Talin alive for his plan to work.*

He had to admit, the Danaan King knew what would drive Lily insane. What would motivate their mother to negotiate. None of them had truly spoiled Lily when she returned, but the idea of losing her again terrified them all. If she could feel the torture Talin went through…Kade shuddered.

The hand that grasped his right arm tightened. "Stop fighting," a voice near him commanded.

"I'm cold," he replied. "I can't help it."

His escort stopped moving. "The surface is straight ahead. We will stay here, make sure you don't lose your way and never make it out." Chadine's voice cut through the darkness. "Deliver His Majesty's message, Fomorian. He is not a patient man. If you wish your future king to remain more or less in one piece, I recommend you don't take side trips to get home."

"I can't see where I'm going. How do you expect me to get out of here?"

He felt her breath brush across his cheek, "Figure it out. Your kind's always had a way of crawling out from the muck."

Hands shoved him forward and he lost his balance.

Instinctively, he tried to move his arms to break his fall. Pain flared in his shoulders and back as his still-bound hands prevented him from doing anything but twisting muscles and joints out of whack. His face and chest scraped against the rough floor as he tumbled forward. The bitter taste of blood filled his mouth.

Grunting, he forced his body up on to his knees. He heard the soft sound of a door closing somewhere behind him. Leaning against the rough stone, he unfolded his legs. The uneven texture of the wall bit into the fresh scrapes and bruises his body had.

"Damnit," he muttered. Fuil had promised to keep Talin alive, but not in once piece. At this point, Kade was convinced that his friend was going to be in a world of pain at the hands of his host.

Like it or not, he had to get back to his parents. Hopefully, his mother was recovered from the attempt on her life. Enough so that she would be able to deal with this situation.

She'd scold him, of course. Not that it mattered. He knew this was his fault. He chose to bring them here, and now Talin was paying for it.

Facing his mother, his Queen, Kade could do. Facing Lily, he wasn't so sure.

Well, you're not going to get anywhere sitting on your ass in a cave, he chided himself. Using the wall, he started to push himself upright. He clenched his teeth as pain erupted across his back, the jagged edges tearing into his flesh.

One particular edge gave him pause. He maneuvered his hands underneath the point, manipulating the rope that bound him against the bottom of the sharp rock. He drew the rope across the rock, sawing at the bindings. He wasn't going to get far in the dark with his hands tied and he knew it. If he could free himself, it would help.

The rope bit into his wrists. Sweat trickled down his face and arms, burning as it hit the open wounds. Kade refused to stop, though. He knew Talin was facing even worse.

His body jerked as the rope finally snapped and his arms came free. Kade moved his arms and shoulders, trying to get rid of the knots in the muscles. Pulling at the remaining rope around his wrists, he took a look around him. A faint light shone to his left. Daylight, perhaps, though it was too dim to know for certain. Right was the way he'd come.

"You don't have a choice," he muttered. "Even if I could find my way back to the city, I wouldn't be any help to him. Not yet."

Reaching out, he put one hand against the cave wall so he'd know if there were any side tunnels, and he started toward the light.

It gradually increased, enough that his eyes adjusted without a problem. When the exit finally came into sight, he stepped up his pace. His soul wanted nothing more than to be out in the open, without the mountain pressing down around him.

A valley opened up before him. For a moment, he considered casting a shadrim to get back. Raising his hand, the fingers shaking from pain, Kade rejected it. There was no guarantee he'd be able to form the right sigil. He was bound to be in trouble for casting the one that got them into this mess. Better to find a horse he could borrow and ride hard.

Dawn was starting to break across the horizon, bathing the valley below in faint light. Kade squinted. A thin column of smoke rose into the air on the far side of the field. Someone lived down there.

Choosing his steps carefully, he made his descent.

What seemed to be hours later, Kade paused. His breath created small clouds in the chill, even though sweat dripped down his back. The thought crossed his mind that Fuil had drugged them somehow. He'd been beaten, yes. Tied up. Dragged through darkness. But he'd never felt this drained before.

The house stood before him. A small cottage with a thatched roof. Vines wove up the sides of the building, while a small fenced garden sat off to one side. The smoke still curled up into the air, promising warmth.

Weariness threatened to overtake him and he staggered toward the door. The world spun as he put his hand on the latch.

***

A woman hummed lightly. The tune slowly worked through the blanket of exhaustion and pain that enveloped him. Kade shifted, feeling a soft mattress beneath his body. He turned his head toward the sound and opened his eyes.

Beyond the alcove where he rested was a large room. A table with chairs sat in the center. The fireplace, large enough to warm the entire house, dominated one wall. She had her back to him, working at a small kitchen area. A black pot, the contents steaming, sat suspended from an iron hook close enough to the fire to cook. A spinning wheel sat in a corner. Baskets of wool on the floor ready to be worked.

Trying not to make a sound, he lifted the blanket covering him.

“I’m not sure you should do that, Your Highness,” the woman said, her back still to him. “I got your clothes washed and mended, but they’re still drying,” One hand, holding a small knife, pointed toward the fire.

Kade shifted his focus and saw his shirt and trousers hanging on a rack near the fire. His boots sat nearby.

Adjusting the blanket, he sat up on one elbow. “I thank you for your kindness, Lady, but I really need—”

She turned to face him. Her weathered face soft but unrelenting. “You really need to stay in bed, Your Highness. Your body is still recovering from whatever you were given. And will be for several hours yet. Your mother, may the Goddess keep her on the throne for years to come, knows where you are. A coach has been dispatched to bring you to them. You are to stay here, recover, until they arrive."

"Where, exactly, is here?"

She put down the knife and scooped a handful of vegetables up. "This is my home. It's not much, but it was enough for me and my husband. He's gone now," she let the vegetables drop into the pot, "so it's just me. I don't mind. I have my craft." She nodded over to the spinning wheel. "It earns me enough to buy what I cannot grow."

"How did you know who I was? I didn't see any other settlements beyond your house."

She looked at him and smiled. "That's no great mystery, Your Highness. My husband used to take care of that house you and your father would go to up the side of the mountain. He taught me what to watch for, so that the room would be ready before you arrived. You and your friend surprised me. The meeting wasn't scheduled for a good two months from now. And I was expecting His Majesty to accompany you both." She paused. "I don't need to know what happened, Your Highness. It's not in my nature to pry. But the creatures living in that mountain are not to be trusted. Too many women have gone for hikes and not returned, for too many years. That they would work such magic on you that they did…I fear for the young Consort. I truly do."

Kade's eyes narrowed. "How do you know about Talin?"

She smiled again, wistfully, "No big secret there. You talk in your sleep. Though I daresay it was more a fever dream over actual rest. Those creatures do not live in the same world as we do. To visit their realm, eat their food, is to invite sickness into your body."

She moved to a cupboard and removed a bowl. As she ladled soup into it, she continued, "I know well what they are. The Tuatha De Danaan. The elves. The mortal enemy of all that is Fomorian. The pact is necessary. I know this. But there are some among their numbers that have broken it numerous times. This new king of theirs is worst of them all. No longer do they wait for hikers to get lost. Now they raid caravans that camp at the mountain's base at nightfall. Goods and people taken away, horses and animals slaughtered. Carts burned." She placed a spoon into the bowl and handed it to Kade. "Eat. You need the strength."

He accepted the bowl, the aroma enticing his stomach. Scooping up a spoonful, he watched her sit at the table. "I knew your husband. I'm sorry for his passing." He blew on the food, then took a bite. The warmth from the stew began to work through his body. "This is really good," he told her, as he scooped up another spoonful. "You said they gave me something that weakened me. Do you know what?"

"No. I'm old, Your Highness, but not that old. My parents came through when we first left Eire. They told me the stories, all of them." She paused, her fingers absently tracing something on the surface of the table, "Their magic is different than ours. We sacrifice our essence, our life itself, to do what we do. And we don't do it often, because of this. Those creatures…they feed off of misery. Off of our magic. They're the reason the Maiten came into being. The first of that lot," she spat on the floor, "went to the Danaans and begged to learn the way of death. Of hatred. Anything you drank, ate, touched even, while in their realm would weaken you. It starts to weave a spell around you within minutes of meeting them. This is why the waystation was created. It was far enough away from the city to keep the taint at bay. At least, that's what Loren always told me. He said he ran into one of them, once, and that it felt like his own life was being siphoned away. They are beautiful and fair to look on, but black and soulless to the core." She leveled a direct stare at Kade. "The longer the Consort remains, the more likely his soul will be tainted. His essence will diminish and turn black. Even if he is returned to the surface, he would be consumed by the evil he's endured. They will delay turning him over, even if their demands are met. Because then they will have control over the Successor through him."

She rose and moved to him. "Rest, Your Highness. It will be a few hours yet before the coach arrives. Even if magic is used to spur it forward." She took the now-empty bowl from him.

Collapsing back on the bed, Kade's mind reeled from her words. If what she said is true, and he suspected it was, this would kill Talin. And Lily. She'd never let someone else control her again. Not after all the pain that Heren and Iris had put her through. Not after the abuse she'd suffered at Erena's hand. She loved Talin—this much Kade knew. But did she love him enough to kill him?

He raised a hand and pushed a hand through his black hair. Pulling it back, he stared at his wrists. They were unmarred and whole. "What?" he started to say, confused.

"I have a member of the royal family collapse on my doorstep and you think I can't be bothered to heal him? You left enough blood on my stoop that'll take years to wash off. I didn't need it staining my best blankets now, did I?"

He felt his eyelids begin to droop again. "You haven't told me your name, good Lady."

Her voice barely penetrated his brain as he drifted off to sleep. "Eilidh."

***

The room was darker when he awoke. The fire still burned, casting flickering light and deep shadows across the room.

"You awake again?" Eilidh asked from the far corner. The soft whirring of her spinning wheel carried across to the alcove where he slept.

"Yeah, I am," Kade replied. "I hate to ask more of you, but my clothes?"

"They're dry and on a chair next to the bed," she replied. "I spin with an eye on the door, not the bed," she continued. "If that makes you more comfortable."

Reaching out his hand, he found the chair she mentioned. He pushed the covers aside and pulled on his breeches. A wave of dizziness threatened to overtake him when he stood. His hand grasped the back of the chair to steady himself. Whatever spell he'd been under, it wasn't completely gone.

He grabbed the shirt and sat in the chair as he put it on. Now that his eyes had adjusted to the dim light, he found his boots nearby. "How long was I asleep?"

"Long enough, I reckon. I imagine the worst of whatever they gave you is gone from your system. The carriage to pick you up should be here soon. I don't recommend you try magic, even if you were inclined to do so. Not until you know your body is clear of the Danaan sorcery."

Kade went to say something when he heard the sound of horses outside. "They're here," Eilidh announced.

A soft glow filled the cottage as she used magic to light dozens of candles at once. She stood, smoothing out the front of her dress. "Enter," she called as someone rapped on the door, then dropped to a deep curtsy.

The door swung open and Corvin entered, followed by Grayson and a few of the household guard. His father nodded at him once. "Kade, are you all right?"

"I'm fine, Father. This woman's the widow of Loren. She's taken good care of me. I would ask that you treat her equally as kind."

Corvin crossed over to the kneeling woman. Taking her hands into his, he raised her up and smiled. “My Lady, I knew your husband well. It saddens me that he has passed this realm. Whatever you ask of the Crown, it will be granted. Both for the years of service given, and the kindness you have shown my son.”

“Your Majesty, I ask no favors. Only that I be allowed to continue his work for you, and the Consort of your Successor. Once he has been recovered, that is.”

Corvin smiled. “Granted, and happily. Though I daresay Her Majesty may insist on increasing your salary and having others come to help you maintain your home. She would not have you repair your roof without someone to hold the ladder.” He looked back at Kade. “But now, I fear we must depart. His Highness is needed if war is to be prevented.”

Kade made his way across the room, holding onto the odd bit of furniture to steady himself. Grayson stepped forward to help but Kade waived him off. “I’m good,” he muttered.

Looking up, he met his father’s calculating gaze. There was a well concealed fury behind those eyes. Kade shifted his focus to the door, unable to withstand the look Corvin gave him.

“Eilidh,” he paused, bowing to his hostess, “I thank you for your hospitality. It was most kind of you, and greatly appreciated.” Whatever else transpired in the coach, his father wouldn’t call him discourteous.

Without another word, Kade walked outside and to the waiting carriage. A guardsman ran before him and opened the door. Grabbing the handle, he took a deep breath before climbing the step and entering.

Two padded benches faced each other. Kade sat on one, preparing himself for the ride to come. Given the anger and fear he saw on his father’s face, he knew it wasn’t going to be a pleasant one.

He heard his father talking to Grayson outside, giving orders to get underway as soon as possible. The door jerked open and Corvin jumped inside. He'd barely sat on the opposite bench before the carriage pulled away.

An uncomfortable silence filled the coach for a few minutes. Kade squirmed, unable to look at his father but knowing he was being studied. "Dad, I don't know what Eilidh's message said, but—"

"It said enough," Corvin snapped. "Of all the stupid things you've done, this one really tops it. I didn't think you'd be dumb enough to fall for something like this, Kade. Let alone take Talin down with you."

Kade looked up. "If we'd stayed there, he would've been thrown into the dungeon for trying to kill the two of you!"

"If you'd stayed, then he wouldn't be in a Danaan dungeon, either!" Corvin paused, "Talin is Lily's Consort, Kade. Use your head. He wouldn't have been put in a cell. At best, he would've been restricted to his rooms. Under guard, but not under arrest. And cleared of any involvement in the plot within a few hours when we found the body! Instead, you bolted like a scared rabbit! Took him someplace neither one of you had ANY reason to go." He took a breath, "Now, you will tell me everything so I can let Her Majesty know where things stand and she can make a decision."

"I can explain it to her…"

"No, Kade. You've overstepped yourself on this one. As a result, Lily's chosen Consort is in danger. The country's on the brink of war. I will tell Her Majesty. You have to try and convince someone else you didn't know how stupid you were being."

"Someone else?" Kade asked.

"You get to tell your sister why you turned the man she loves over to the elves. I will not spare you that conversation. Now, I have to know everything that happened. From the beginning."

Kade swallowed hard and started to talk.

Chapter Nine

He was cold. And stiff. Those were the first things that Talin thought when he regained consciousness. Whatever he was laying on was hard and unyielding. He rolled over onto his back, hands going to the surface beneath him. Rough stone, and a few bits of straw. He tried opening his eyes, but only one obeyed. His fingers probed at the other, felt the swollen socket. *Great*, he thought.

The room was bare stone with a single door set into a wall of bars. The dungeon, then. A stone glowed down a hallway, the light barely reaching his cell.

He touched his ribcage, wincing at a few places. Bruised, possibly broken, and an eye that was swollen shut. His fingers brushed against his neck. An iron gorget circled his throat. He felt the first few links of chain running from the back of the band.

Carefully, Talin shifted again, trying to make out where the chain ended in the dim light. An iron bar rested at the base of the closest wall. A single link ran through it. He reached out and grasped the chain, pulling on it slightly. The sound of metal against metal echoed in the chamber. Moving onto his knees, he started to calculate the amount of freedom in his cage he really had. It wasn't much. He wouldn't even be able to stand upright.

He leaned against the wall, one arm draped against his knee, and tried to clear his head. The news of his father's race, and that he was half Danaan, sat like a lump of iron in his stomach. There was no way he could be related to these…creatures. He was everything they weren't. At least, that's what he told himself.

Absently, he reached out with his other hand and began to twist at the silver ring he'd worn since his mother had died. The only time he'd ever taken it off was to give to

Rylin last spring, as a message to Lily that he was coming for her.

His left eye began to itch, then burn. Without thinking, he placed his palm to the area. As soon as the ring came in contact with his skin, the burning stopped. A wave of coolness washed over him. He lowered his hand, and blinked.

The swelling was gone.

As his vision cleared, he saw a shadow outside his cell shift. "Who's there?" he called out.

A young girl, her face smudged with dirt, pressed her face against the bars, "It's just me, milord. I ain't nobody."

Talin smiled a little, his jaw aching at the movement. "You're not nobody. You're someone. What's your name?"

"They never gave me one. Just call me 'mongrel' and 'rat'."

"Those aren't good names."

The child looked at him. "What's your name?"

"Talin."

"You're like me, aren't you?"

"I don't know. What do you mean?"

"My poppa wasn't from here. He looked ugly. That's why they call me mongrel. Said I look like him and not like momma." The child's face grew sad. "She's really pretty. I'm not."

"Nonsense, I think you look just fine." Talin watched the girl's face light up. "Would it be okay if I gave you a name?"

"Maybe. What would it be?"

Talin bit his lip, trying to look like he was thinking of a good name for the girl. "What about…Myrena?"

The girl grinned. "I like that."

He smiled back at her, "Good. Myrena it is. Now, Myrena, can you help me?"

The creaking of a door opening echoed down the hallway. Talin saw the panicked look on the girls' face. "Go," he told her. "Hide." She scurried off into the dark while he took a few deep breaths. Whoever was coming probably wasn't there to unlock his chain.

Four guards escorted a cloaked figure. From the way they moved, he figured it was a woman. He kept his face impassive. Whatever Fuil wanted, he wasn't ready to hand it over easily. No matter who he sent here to torture him.

One man lifted a set of keys off an iron hook set into the wall opposite his cell door. Twisting it in the lock, he cautioned, "We got him chained by the neck, Your Highness. And the chain's not got a lot of length. As long as you stay near the door, he can't reach you."

The hooded figure nodded before stepping into the cell. She turned and said something, but it was too low for Talin to hear. Whatever it was, it made her escort lock the door, replace the key, and walk away. Not too far. He could still see them down the hall. But it was far enough to give the semblance of privacy.

He turned his attention back to his visitor, and waited.

The woman raised her hands and pushed back the hood of the cloak. Adrenalin surged through him as he recognized the face.

"Well, well. How the mighty have fallen," Iris mocked him.

"What do you want, Iris?" He didn't bother to hide his disgust.

She smiled at him. It came across like a predator looking at its prey. "Want? Oh, I want quite a bit. And you're going to give it to me."

"Not likely. But you've been delusional for a while now. I'd be more surprised if you said you didn't want anything." He saw a flicker of anger play across her face.

Good, he thought. The more calm and complacent he could be, at least outwardly, the more it was going to irritate her. Small pleasure, to be sure, but right now the only good thing that'd happened in the last day or so.

"Too bad you missed Kade, Iris," he continued. "I'm sure he'd have loved to have a pointed discussion with you. I hope you brought some good shoes. Because you won't be able to outrun him much longer."

He watched the muscles on her jaw flex. Her eyes narrowed, "I don't care. By the time I'm done with you, he won't be able to touch me." The predatory grin returned to her face. "You all think you're so smart, finding Lily. Shielding her from criticism and realities of life. It's time for her to grow up and see that life's not all rainbows and waterfalls. If she's going to rule Tiadar, so be it. But I'm going to teach her a lesson. Make her understand what it's like to live with the constant reminder of someone else."

Talin shook his head, "I don't get it, Iris. Why do you hate her so much? Her parents took you in, raised you! What happened to you?"

"She came back, that's what happened to me!" Iris snapped. She started to pace, "You all think it was so great and wonderful to get her back. But I was shoved aside like trash! No one bothered to ask me if I wanted to be replaced! Instead of congratulating me for finding her, I got ignored! Shoved aside! It was as if I never was part of the family!"

"You're wrong. So very wrong. I was there. I saw you at every meal. With few exceptions, when the four of them were trying to figure out how to be a family again, you were part of it. No one shoved you aside. You offered up your room, your clothes! Nobody took anything from you." Talin looked at her, confused.

She stopped pacing and moved toward him. Even in the dim light, he could see the hatred on her face. "She took my life from me, Talin. I went from being someone to no one. I wasn't the princess anymore. I was thrown aside, discarded, same as I was the night my mother was murdered. Those first few nights, right after Lily was taken, I was forgotten. Then everyone started to love me again. As the months turned into years and she was still gone, I got to take her place. *I was their daughter*! And then you came to Kade, told us you found her. I couldn't stop him from casting that shadrim to get her. And I hoped, foolishly, that everything would be the same. Only it wasn't. Because then she took *you*, too." Iris knelt next to him, the back of her hand stroking his cheek.

Talin resisted the urge to push her hand away, knowing it would only anger her more. Iris loved him? When? He caught her hand by wrist, holding it gently. "Iris, you know as well as I do that we can't choose who we love. I only ever saw you as a friend, and a part of the family I swore an oath to protect. What I feel for Lily goes beyond reason, beyond words. There will never come a day that I will choose you over her."

"That may be, Talin. But you will give me something. And it will be a constant reminder to Lily that your words and deeds are quite different things."

A cold feeling of dread washed across him. "I'm not going to give you anything."

Iris reached out a single finger and began to trace the line of his collarbone, sending a shiver of fear down his spine. "Oh, yes you will. Because my friends out there are going to come in here when I tell them to." Her voice almost purred. Talin's skin shrank away from her touch, revulsion mixing with panic in his mind. "And they're going to put something into your veins that'll make your body do exactly what I want it to do. But you won't be able to stop me. You'll remember it, each and every time. And it's going to keep happening until I know I carry your child in me." He slammed his body against the wall, trying to move away from her. Iris grinned at him, "And, then, when the child is born, I'll send it to Court. Where Lily can watch it grow up near its father. And every time Lily reads your mind through that link of yours, she'll see you and me together. She may make you her Consort, but I'll be there with both of you every time you kiss. Every time you make love to her. I'll be there. And she'll know you're thinking of me, not her." She leaned in, her lips brushing against his.

Bile rose in his stomach as he jerked away. The chain around his neck prevented him from moving far. Iris' laughter rang in his ears. Talin knew how much that would hurt Lily. And how, no matter how much he told her differently, Lily would have a problem believing him.

She rose. The predatory smile got wider. "Now you're starting to understand, Talin. Guards!" she called out.

They rushed over to the door, "Yes, Your Highness?"

"It's time for you to give the Consort his medicine."

One of them reached back and pulled the keys off the ring again. Panicking, Talin tried to rise, to prepare himself to fight, but the chain jerked him off balance and he fell back to the stone floor. Coughing, he pushed himself off the ground. Strong hands grabbed his arms and rolled him over. A third guard, a clear vial and needle in his hands, hovered near the door. "Hold him still," he instructed the three guards who held him.

Talin fought back, struggling against them as they pinned him to the floor. Two of the guards knelt on his arms, forcing him to lay flat. The other grasped his ankles. He screamed once, as he felt the needle pierce his skin.

Iris' laughter echoed in Talin's ears.

Chapter Ten

"Lily! Wait!" Kade called out, desperate to stop her. She didn't pause though, and the door slammed behind her.

He sank into a chair. Dejected, he put his head in his hands. Telling her was one of the hardest things he'd dealt with. The shock, horror, and fear that played across her face as he told her everything that'd happened to him and Talin since they'd left cut deep. He couldn't answer her last question. How Talin was when he was taken away, set free. Simply that the last sight he had of her fiancée was him being driven to the ground from a blow to the jaw. Her face had grown pale and she fled from the room.

"Give her time, Kade. She's got to adjust to the news." Rylin spoke softly from behind his chair.

"Talin doesn't have time, though." He stared into the fire, guilt chewing at his gut. "I should've found a way back down there, Rylin. Done something more than just left him there."

Her hands gently kneaded at his shoulders. Reaching up, he held one of her hands and caressed it with his finger. "No, Kade. You did what you had to do. Come back, deliver the message. You said yourself, Fuil wants to use him. He has to keep Talin alive."

"Alive, yes. But I'm not at all certain he'll be treated well. If I was that sick after the short time I spent in the mountain, I can't imagine how he'll be when he comes out. He may not be the man I remember. The one Lily loves. If that's the case, I'll never forgive myself."

She moved in front of him, kneeling where he had to see her face. "Then we help him remember who he is. Everyone in your family did this for Lily, when she came home. They'll do the same for Talin."

Kade looked away, unable to meet the intense look in her eyes. "I don't think it'll be that easy, Rylin. I know he's got a strong mind. He's going to be able to take a lot. But the Danaans…they hate us. It runs so deep. It's like the stories about Eire have come to life. I don't think it'll stop with a treaty. They won't rest until every single Fomorian is dead. And they'll start with him. They'll execute him in front of Lily."

"Not if I have anything to say about it." Keryth replied.

Kade jumped up, twisting, to face his mother. He swallowed hard. "I, um, didn't hear you come in," he stammered.

"Rylin, would you give me a moment with my son? Lily's calmer, but could use you right now."

"Of course, Your Majesty." She curtsied and started to leave the room.

Keryth reached out an arm and stopped her. "My dear, you'll be my daughter soon enough. I think, once this knot is untangled, the country could use something good to celebrate. You can drop the formalities when we're alone."

"Thank you," Rylin glanced back at Kade, smiling. "Be nice to him. He's beating himself up worse than anything you could do to him." Turning, she walked out of the room and closed the door behind her.

Kade stood there, unsure what to say. He'd gone over everything that'd happened in the carriage ride with Corvin. Certainly it'd been relayed to her. Unless she was here to tell him what would happen to him, Kade wasn't sure what she could want from him.

"I'm not here to scold you, Kade. I'm certain your father did that already. And Rylin was right. There's nothing I could say or do to you right now to make you regret your decision any more than you already do. That being said—" she paused "—we still need to talk. Sit."

Kade did as he was commanded, easing his body back into the chair. His muscles still ached from both the beating and the invasive nature of being among the Danaans. Eilidh had cured the outer wounds. The ones that scarred his soul, however, would take a lot longer to heal.

He watched as his mother settled into a chair near him. “I heard the story from your father. Is there anything you’ve left out?”

“No,” he replied. “I told him everything we saw, what we were told. I think I even told him about the food we ate.” He leaned back, letting his head rest against the high back of the chair. “I don’t think Fuil’s going to be happy with a new treaty, no matter what it says. He wants us dead, all of us. There was none of the ease that Kronos had in her nature, the inner peace. Fuil didn’t know us, but hated us based on us being Fomorian. Any meeting you have with him will be a trap. I know it.”

“And you think he’s using Talin as bait?”

“I know he is. He’s using Talin to get to Lily. Because he believes you’ll do anything to keep her happy after all those years without her.”

Keryth leaned forward, “Kade, your father mentioned something about their dead being encased in crystal. That there was a man there, the same one that Talin claimed was at the banquet. The one that said he was his father. Did you see this body?”

“I saw…someone. I didn’t get up close enough to look.” He paused, “Something about it wasn’t right. I don’t think that was Talin’s father. Either the body in the crystal or the man at coronation.”

“I agree. We found a body, after the rubble was cleared. The would-be assassin wasn’t able to escape his own cleverness.” There was a sadness to her voice.

Kade waited for her to continue. The fire popped, breaking up the stillness in the room.

"It was Heren, Kade. How he escaped his prison is already under investigation. Grayson found him, all but crushed to death. He was mad. His last words, after hearing he'd failed, were 'You only think I did. The might of the Tuatha de Danaan will rise. Iris will bring down Talin. And, through him, Lily. Even if Keryth wins the battle, Fuil will win the war'." She paused again. "You were right; it was elvish magic that was used. Both to hide Heren's identity, and make us forget he was even there." The gaze she leveled at Kade made him squirm. "Which makes your actions in taking Talin there all the more dangerous. I understand why, to a degree. Now, did you have any inclination Iris was there? See someone that could've been her walking away from you?"

He searched through his memories, trying to scrutinize every single detail he could recall. "No," he replied. "Nothing. Outside of Fuil and two others, they were all guards. No one else said a word. The two we did talk to weren't Iris. I know that."

She nodded, "I'm not surprised. If she's there, she'd stay hidden until the time was right." Sighing, she leaned back in her chair. "I don't know what she wants, Kade. I really don't. It was as if she shut herself away from us after Lily came back. Your father noticed it, tried to talk to her. But she laughed him off. Said he should stop worrying and go enjoy having his daughter back. But, whatever it is, she's willing to destroy all of Tiadar to get it. And I can't let that happen."

"So, how do we do this? Save Talin and avoid a war at the same time?"

"War, I fear, is inevitable. The Tuatha have done things that go against the treaty. Like kidnapping women and men, charming them, mixing the races together to increase their own population. The only reason Aeowolf relented to Cerridwen's plea was because the Tuatha that were to come swore to stay apart. Fomorian and Danaan magic does not work together. It's as much at odds with each other as we are as a people. Heren was dead before the explosion. He just didn't know it."

"Is there any truth to what Fuil said? That Talin's father was Danaan? Or was it a ruse to get us someplace he could take us prisoner at?"

"His father wasn't Danaan. At least, I don't believe he was. And that's where I need you, Kade. Tomorrow, we're heading back to the mountain. I'm taking your father with me, but not Lily. I want you to take her and Rylin and head to Isanne's Well. That's where I remember Rose, Talin's mother, said she was from. If you find her family, they may remember Talin's father. See if you can find out who the man was, what happened to him."

Kade leaned forward, "Why would he say anything about the woman if it wasn't true?"

"There was a woman, yes, that Kronos asked your father to take with him. It wasn't Talin's mother." Her voice rang with conviction.

"Whose mother was it, then? Someone we know?"

She shifted, and Kade narrowed his gaze. It wasn't like her to be evasive. Diplomatic, yes. But he'd never known her to deflect questions.

"If I tell you, it doesn't go beyond this room unless absolutely necessary. Only tell Talin if you need to, to put his mind to ease. As to Lily," she paused, "I'll tell her myself. This whole business may make it irrelevant soon, anyway."

"Iris?" he asked, his voice hushed.

She nodded. "The woman was my sister. She and Jasper were married, but it wasn't a good one. She left him and was making her way to Lyvanna Keep. The weather turned bad, so she took refuge in a cave. She went to sleep. The next thing she remembered was waking up with me next to her, scared out of my mind. They'd erased all memory of her time with them. She was frightened for the baby, was certain Jasper would want to take it from her. A friend of ours since childhood came forward, offered to marry her and claim the child was his. He'd always loved her. The ruse worked. At least, we thought it did. She grew to love him, and they'd just shared that Iris would have a baby brother or sister when they were murdered. It wasn't until months later that we realized it was all a distraction so Erena could get away with Lily. The assassin went as far as sending Iris down the hall, her nightgown stained with blood, so we'd all panic. The guards outside the nursery where you two slept were doubled. We never thought Erena would do what she did."

"So, Iris is part Danaan? Jasper wasn't her father?"

"We don't know, Kade. Jasper says she's his. I can accept that, if she does. But, after what she did to Lily…drugging all of us that night. I tried to raise her the same as you. Treat her like my own child. Something's consuming her, Kade. There's an evil in her, a darkness that could be Danaan in origin. If she and I come face to face, when this is over, maybe I'll find out the truth. The path she's walking now… I fear the next time I see her will be after she's dead."

An idea started to form in Kade's mind. "You want Fuil to think he's right. That Talin's half Danaan."

Keryth nodded. "I think that may be the only thing that'll keep Talin alive until we can get him back. Talin's going to be King, when I'm gone. Fuil probably plans to control what's left of our people through him. Get Lily to agree to anything, in order to keep Talin alive. Yes, we're going to talk. I'll entertain the idea of a new treaty. If only to see for myself what condition Talin's in." Kade drew back from the look that crossed her face. "I've discussed this with Lily, Kade. And this is why she's to go with you to Isanne's Well. If I feel Talin is beyond saving, we will have no choice."

"You'd kill him?" The question came out as a whisper. "After everything he's done, what he's going through now? You'd do that to him? To Lily?"

"Yes, I would. Because I will not hand rule of Tiadar over to the Tuatha de Danaans. I *cannot* do that." She rose. "Get some sleep, Kade. You ride at first light. Your job, besides finding out what you can about Talin's father, is to keep your sister as far from the Elivin mountains as you can."

Chapter Eleven

Talin crawled to the farthest corner that the chain would allow and retched. The drug they'd given him was subsiding, and his stomach was unrelenting in the need to get rid of it in some way. If only his mind could purge its contents as readily.

The spasms subsided after a few minutes. He knew he couldn't escape the smell entirely, but he moved away and leaned against the wall. He could still smell Iris on his skin. The first thing on his list, after he got out of here, was a bath. Though he wasn't sure he'd ever really feel clean again.

Iris had left him a few hours ago, promising to come back again 'soon'. The guards trailed after her. The first thing he'd done when he could control his body again was find his clothes.

At least she hadn't taken those from him.

"I'm sorry, Lily," he whispered. "I tried to fight, but it wasn't good enough."

"Who's Lily?" A small voice called out from the shadows.

Talin squinted, finally seeing Myrena hiding near the door of his cell. "Myrena? Is that you? I can't see you."

She moved into the light. "Who's Lily?"

"Lily's someone I love very much."

"What's she like?"

"She's really kind, and smart. She's got dark hair, just like you."

"She sounds nice. Do you miss her?"

"More than you can imagine. I think I even miss her when I'm sleeping."

"How much?'

"How much what?"

"How much do you love her?"

Talin smiled at her, “Enough that I never want to hurt her. But I’m afraid I did.”

“You didn’t hurt anybody. That mean lady hurt you. If Lily loves you, she’ll know that. You just gotta tell her about the medicine they gave you.”

Something about Myrena’s confidence warmed Talin’s soul. “You may be right about that, my friend. But I can’t tell Lily that while I’m here. And that lady wants to come back and hurt me again.”

“That’s sad. I don’t like watching people get hurt.”

He glanced up at the wall across from his cell. The keys hung on the hook. “Myrena, can you help me?”

“I can try.”

“There’s some keys on a ring up there,” he pointed at the wall. “Can you reach those and slide them in here? Maybe one will fit this,” he touched the ring that circled his neck. “I can’t even stand up all the way and my legs are awfully sore.”

She looked at the keys then back at him. “But those might open the door, too. And then you’d run away and I wouldn’t see you again.”

“You could come with me. I’m betting someone as smart as you even knows how to get to the surface.”

Her eyes got wide, “Really? You’d let me come with you?”

Smiling, he said, “Yes. If you helped me, got us up to the surface, I’d take you to meet Lily. She knows how to make this drink. She calls it ‘hot chocolate’. And it’s really good.”

“How good?”

“It’s one of the best things you’ll ever drink. And I’ve drunk a lot of different things.” He looked at her. “Please, Myrena. If I don’t get out of here, that lady’s going to keep hurting me. And then she’ll hurt Lily. I don’t want that to happen. But I can’t do it without your help.”

Myrena stood up and moved to stand right below the rings. One arm reached up the wall, then stopped. "You promise you'll take me with you, right? And that I'll get hot chocolate?"

"As much as you can drink. I promise."

Without a sound, she pulled the keys off the hook. Talin shifted, crawling as far forward as the chain let him. He held out one hand, "That's great, Myrena. Now, put them on the ground and push them through far enough for me to reach them."

He tried to stay calm as she moved slowly, making sure the keys didn't rattle. Glancing down the hallway, his ears strained to hear anyone coming. "That's it, just push them hard at me now," he coaxed her.

The keys moved inside, just out of his reach. Thinking quickly, he shifted his position and used the heel of his boot to hook the ring and bring it within reach of his hands. "Thank you," he told her. His fingers fumbled in haste, flipping through the keys. He isolated one from the others, the one that looked most likely able to unlock the chain around his neck. Reaching his hands around to the back of his head, he searched for the lock.

It seemed like forever until he heard a soft click and the metal gorget came loose. Resisting the urge to throw it aside, he instead laid it carefully on the floor. Scrambling to his feet, he took a moment to stretch. The knots in his back protested, but it felt good to stand fully. Talin reached through the bars and started to work on the lock to his cage. Adrenaline surged through his body. *Don't screw this up,* he told himself. *You're almost free. Or closer to it than you've been for a few days.*

The tumbler moved. The sound echoed off the stone walls. He threw a worried glance at the hallway, his ears alert for any alarm. He let go of the ring and brought his arm back through, then eased the door open enough to move his body through. For a moment, he considered locking the cage again and putting the keys back. Instead, he turned to his rescuer. “Lead the way,” he whispered. “But we have to be fast. And quiet.”

She smiled, nodded, and beckoned him forward. “I know a tunnel,” Myrena replied. “It’s small in places, and long, but it goes all the way out of the mountain.”

He dared one more look back, over his shoulder, and followed his small guide.

She stopped a few moments later, at a dead end. His eyes scanned the wall in the dim light, “Where do we go from here, Myrena?” he asked. The rush of escape fading as panic threatened to take over.

“Down here,” she said.

Talin looked down and saw her pulling a stone out of the wall where it met the floor. Her small body slid through easily. It was going to be a tight fit for him. “Don’t worry,” she called out. “It’s bigger on the other side. I can close it after you’re in here.”

Going back wasn’t an option. There was no way he was going to let Iris dig her talons into him any deeper. He dropped to the floor and wormed his way into the opening. His shoulders scraped painfully against the stone, but he clawed his way forward. A few feet in, he felt the passage open up. With a grunt, he pulled his hips through and free. Talin twisted, sitting down, and pulled his feet clear. He couldn’t see his hand in front of his face, but heard Myrena scurry back down the hole. The scraping of stone echoed in the small antechamber and the meager light that traveled down the tunnel disappeared as she shut the door.

“This way,” she commanded.

“Myrena, wait. I can’t see.”

“Why not?”

“I wasn’t raised here. On the surface, we have light from the sun, from candles and lanterns. I’m not used to seeing in the dark. Not this kind of dark, anyway,”

He felt a small hand grasp his. “It’s okay. Don’t be scared. I’ll lead you.” She tugged at his hand.

Talin stood, one hand raised to gauge the height of the room. It was a little taller than him, but not by much. Myrena pulled at his hand again.

She led him through a maze, turning at random. Or so it seemed to him. He completely lost any sense of where he was, or where they were going. She moved slowly at first, making sure he stayed with her. His eyes adjusted eventually, making it so he could at least make out her form as she moved in front of him.

“Myrena,” he said, “can we stop for a few minutes? I’m not feeling good.”

She turned and looked up at him. “What’s wrong?”

A wave of nausea hit him, forcing him to lean against the wall for support. Sweat trickled down his back. “I’m not sure. I think it’s from the medicine they gave me.” He took a few deep breaths in an attempt to quell the queasiness.

“Not here,” she said. “But soon. We’re not at the surface yet. We have to get to a safe spot first.” Urgency colored her voice.

He felt weak. His head spun, but he pushed away from the wall and trailed behind his guide.

The air in the tunnel was hot, oppressive. His lungs began to hurt with every breath he took. Sweat seeped into his eyes, stinging as he blinked.

“Not much farther. I promise. This is the worst part.” Myrena urged him forward.

“Where are we?” he gasped.

“Near the heart of the mountain,” she replied. She moved close enough that he could see her face. Her hair hung in damp clumps from her head. “You have to keep moving,” she said as she pulled at his hand.

Resolutely, he gathered his strength. *Just put one foot in front of the other*, he told himself.

Time stood still. Talin couldn't think about what day it was, let alone the hour. His sense of that had disappeared when Kade first led him into the mountain. Had it been one day, or a week? Was his friend back with Lily now, or struggling to find the surface like he was?

Was Lily still looking for him, or had she given him up for dead?

His lungs started to spasm, the coughing fit making him drop to his knees. That's when he felt it. The slight whiff of cooler, fresher air. Staggering to his feet, he put both hands on the walls that surrounded him and willed himself forward.

"That's it, Talin," Myrena's voice called out from the darkness ahead of him. "We're almost someplace safe, where you can rest."

He blinked, his vision blurred. The way ahead looked slightly brighter. He staggered toward the light, only to collapse into darkness.

***

His mind started to sort through images as he woke. The sound of a cart in motion, the sensation of being carried. A damp cloth on his head, cutting through the fever that raged in his body. His chest hurt, but the air smelled sweet and fresh. He tried to put an order to the information but gave up. Whatever had happened, wherever he was now, wasn't another cell. The bed beneath him cradled him gently.

Talin kept his eyes shut and listened for clues. There was someone else nearby, possibly in another room given how muffled the sound was. They shuffled more than stepped.

He shifted, testing his body. *Good*, he thought, *I'm not tied to the bed.* A small measure of safety to be sure, but an important one. Whoever was out there didn't see him as a threat. Or as an escaped prisoner who needed to be returned.

Myrena!

He bolted upright, his eyes wide open, and instantly regretted the movement. His lungs spasmed and coughing racked his body, leaving him weak. He fell back onto the bed when it passed. It wasn't dark, but the light still stung his eyes enough to make him squint.

The room was small, sparsely furnished. The bed, a small chest, a single chair, and the table next to him. Everything was simply made, utilitarian.

A single window sat high on the wall, the thin fabric curtain filtering the light. Sunlight, he hoped. It was a good indication they'd made it out of the mountain, anyway. Some clothes sat on the chair. But Myrena was nowhere in sight.

He lay there, letting his eyes adjust. Slowly, he rose and reached for the clothes. They were big, but would work. He was pulling the shirt over his head when the door opened.

Talin stopped, the shirt halfway down his chest, and stared. An older man, his hair white, stood in the door with a tray. "You're awake," he said.

"Yeah," Talin replied, letting the shirt fall into place. "Though I'm not sure where I am, for one."

The man slid the tray onto the table. "You're in my home. It's not much, but you and your young friend will be safe while you recover."

"Myrena's here?"

"Is that her name? She wouldn't tell me." The man laughed.

"I need to leave," Talin said as he started to rise from the bed.

The man put a hand on his shoulder, pushing him back down. "Not yet. You're still recovering. Anyone who goes through what you did needs to get their strength back before moving forward. I'd just be finding you in a ditch somewhere between here and town otherwise."

"You don't understand—"

"Yes, I do. You're Talin. And were held captive by the creatures in the mountain. Your little friend told me that much." For a second, his gaze shifted to Talin's hand, then he looked back at him. "And I can figure out the rest of it. The creatures won't come here looking for you. Too open. I'm far enough away from where I found you both that they won't come here." He paused. "Eat. I'll send Myrena in here. She's been worried sick for the last two days." He turned and reached for the door latch.

"Two days?" Talin stared at him, trying to mentally reconcile the furtive dreams and passage of time. "I was out that long?"

"That I know of, yes. I don't know how long the two of you sat in that cave. You'd have to ask your friend that one. It was sheer luck that thunderstorm caught me on the way home. Otherwise, I'd have never found you."

"Thank you..." Talin let his voice trail off, uncertain what his rescuer's name was.

"Name's Tennet. I'll be back for the dishes in a bit." He opened the door and left, closing it behind him.

Talin rose and went to the tray. Some bread, meat, and vegetables greeted him. It wasn't much, but his stomach growled in anticipation. His hands shook slightly as he picked up the tray and moved back to the bed. *No wonder you're weak*, he told himself, *it's been at least three days since you ate anything. Not since that dinner with Fuil and Kade.* He picked up the bread and took a small bite. His body screamed at him to devour it immediately, but he took his time. He'd heard stories of people who got sick if they ate too quickly after days of fasting.

He was using the last of the bread to sop up the juices when someone knocked on the door. “Talin?” Myrena called out.

“Come in,” he said, then popped the last morsel in his mouth.

The door swung open enough for her to slide in. “Tennet said you were awake, but that I had to wait for you to eat.” Her voice was timid.

“It’s fine, Myrena. I’m fine. Or, I will be. I owe you a debt, my friend. You got me out of there.”

“Will you still take me to see your friend Lily?”

Talin smiled at her. “Of course I will. And she’ll make you lots of hot chocolate.”

She grinned.

“Can you tell me what happened? I don’t know how we got here.”

“We were near the cave…the one that opened to the surface…when you got sick. You fell over and wouldn’t wake up. I tried to wake you up, but you wouldn’t, so I moved you a little bit. I thought you might be thirsty, so I went to find a spring I knew was nearby. I found Tennet instead. He’s like you, from the surface. He said he could help you. So I brought him to you. He gave you some water and did something else that made you throw up but not wake up.” She paused, “I got scared when he said he had to bring you here. I never went out of the cave before. We waited for the storm to pass and then he promised he’d make sure I stayed safe too. He’s been really nice since we got here, but I feel better now that you’re awake.”

“So do I, Myrena.” Talin laughed. “We may have to sneak out of here, though. Tennet wants me to stay longer, but I think I’m okay now.”

“Promise you won’t leave without me?”

“I promise.”

Talin rose and went to pick up the tray. The dishes rattled softly as his hands shook, but he held onto it. “Can you open the door for me?” he asked.

The girl nodded and swung the door open wide. Talin walked out into the common room.

Tennet rose from a chair near the fire. “You’re not ready for that yet, my boy,” he said as he took the tray from Talin. “Sit,” he thrust his chin toward the seats.

Talin did as he was told, but tried to brush it off. “I’m not that sick, Tennet. I’m sure Myrena and I can be on our way soon.”

“You honestly think I’d let the Consort wander about sick? The Queen would have my hide.” He kept his back to Talin.

“You know who I am, then?”

“Like I told you before, she told me your name. I put the rest together.” He turned around and gave Talin a direct look. “Don’t know how you got lost in that mountain, or what those creatures did to you. Don’t need to know. But I won’t have no royalty think I wasn’t hospitable.”

“I promise, Tennet, I won’t accuse you of mistreatment. That you let me have a bed and nursed me through that fever was beyond any measure of hospitality I could ask for. But it’s not in me to lounge around idle, either.”

“I’ll make you a deal. I’ve got a pile of logs out back. Been delaying cutting it up for the coming winter. The day you can go out there, split it, and stack it without falling over is the day I say you’re healthy enough to leave here. I’ll even give you both a ride into town in the wagon afterwards. But not before.”

Talin took a look at his host. Tennet stood there, impassive. It’d been all that he could do to walk out from the bedroom to the chair without collapsing. Like it or not, Tennet was right. He wasn’t in any shape to put up a fight.

Leaving here before he was strong enough would only put him and Myrena right back into danger. “Agreed.”

Chapter Twelve

Talin brought the axe down on the log, letting the momentum of the swing do most of the work. The log split into pieces. He leaned the axe against the old trunk and picked up the wood. He slid the smaller bits into place on the growing stack.

He gave his body a day of rest—that was it. Then he came out and started to work. That first day was slow. When he finally gave up, he couldn't tell he'd made much of a dent in the pile of logs waiting. Now, though, the stacked firewood was overtaking the shelter and he could see that the end was near.

An end to recovery, and the chance to make his way into town. Back to Lily.

Tennet had been a gracious host. He made a few small toys for Myrena in the evening hours, when it was too dark out to work. Kept them fed. He insisted Talin keep the bed, though. Some nonsense about him being royalty.

A rivulet of sweat ran down from his forehead, dropping off his nose. *Right now*, he thought, *I'm about as royal as a skunk. Probably smell like one, too.*

He turned around and saw Myrena staring at something in the grass. She'd amazed him, to be honest. Once she got over her initial fear, the surface world he knew was full of wonders for her. And she'd embraced the chance to learn. He grabbed the axe on his way past the stump. Tennet said no one came this way, but Talin wasn't entirely convinced of that.

"Myrena, what is it?" he called out to her as he headed her way.

"Just some weird stones. They have stuff on them."

Talin relaxed a little. Coming up beside her, he saw two small headstones. "Those are grave markers, Myrena.

Someone who lived with Tennet died and this is his way of remembering them."

She turned her head sideways, "What's the markings on them for?"

He knelt down to be closer to her level. "That's writing he carved into the stone. It tells you their names and when they died." He glanced at her, "When we get to town, I'll start to teach you to read."

"Okay. But can you tell me what they say now?"

"Sure. This one—" he pointed to the one on the left "—has the name of Aislynn. Says they died about five years ago. And this one—" he reached out and brushed some dead grass off the stone. "—is for someone named Rose. And that she died about fifteen years ago." His voice trailed off as he saw some smaller words carved below the date.

"Myrena, child, could you go inside the house?" Tennet's voice was low.

Talin rose and looked at the older man as Myrena ran off. "Were you ever going to tell me?" he asked.

"Tell you what? That we were stupid parents because she fell for a peddler? That we drove her away by forbidding her to see him? We didn't know she was pregnant, Talin. She didn't tell us. She left to be with him, that's all we knew."

"How about that you were my grandfather!" Anger boiled up inside him.

"To be honest, I didn't know how to tell you. We didn't do right by your mother. Saw that as soon as she didn't come back. Saw the peddler again the next season, asked about her. He said she'd up and left him, but didn't know where she went to. By the time we heard anything about you, your past, and figured it out it seemed a little late. Aislynn thought we'd be seen as nothing more than people who wanted to exploit you for your connection to the royal family." He nodded at Talin. "When your friend found me, talked me into helping, I was going to get you into town as soon as I could. I saw your ring when I loaded you into my cart. Knew who you were then, and that I wasn't going to let you leave until I knew you could handle yourself again."

"What's my ring got to do with anything?"

"I made it for her. I sent it with a letter once, apologizing for what happened. I never got an answer. Figured she didn't want us to be part of your lives at that point."

Talin stood there, the anger giving way to a sense of relief. "You knew my father, then?"

"Yes. Still never liked him, thought Rose could've done better. He came back one or two more summers after she left, then stopped. Heard he swindled someone in town and ended up meeting the hangman for his trouble." He started to walk back to the house. Talin fell in step beside him. "She was extremely loyal. To her friends, the people she loved. When she decided she loved this peddler, that was it. Once she made up her mind, she never changed it. Even after she left him, she still loved him. Chances are, she loved you more and that's what drove her away. He had some bad habits, ones she wouldn't have wanted you to grow up around."

Closing his eyes for a moment, Talin gave in to the relief. His father wasn't Danaan, no matter what Fuil had insisted. "I've got to get back, though. I can't stay here. Come with me. Or, at least promise to come once this knot is unraveled. I want you to meet Lily."

"I may do that once, but home's here for me. The whole Court thing isn't what I like. That one," he pointed at Myrena as she chased a butterfly, "needs stability. If you have too much going on, send her back here. I'd like the chance to get it right."

"I'll think on it," Talin replied. "But I also promised her a few things. You wouldn't have me go back on a promise, would you?"

"No, not that. And I promised you a trip into town when you were done with my firewood." He glanced up at the sky. "It's not quite mid-day. If we get the wagon hitched up, we can be at the inn in time for supper. Get you some real food, not the slop I cook."

Talin laughed, "It's been fine." Pausing, he took a breath. "Would it be all right with you if I called you Grandfather?"

The older man sniffed, "Only if you don't expect me to put on airs. Don't need none of the townfolk thinking I'm anything different because my grandson's the Consort now."

"Nah, we wouldn't want that." Talin put his arm around his back as they walked toward the house.

An hour later, Talin pulled himself into the seat of the wagon. Looking back over his shoulder, he asked Myrena, "All settled?"

She nodded, excitement dancing on her pale face.

He looked back at his grandfather and said, "Let's go."

Tennet snapped the reins and the cart jerked forward.

***

Iris strode through the hallway leading to Talin's cell. Fuil had left him in an unused section, which was just fine for her. He should be isolated. It would make him start to look forward to her company, even if he hated what she did to him.

Not that it mattered to her. He was a means to an end. If she couldn't destroy Lily, she'd make sure any relationship she had with Talin would be tenuous. Iris knew

Lily well enough that the wench wouldn't ever trust Talin again, not when she was through with him.

Add to that having to see his bastard child at Court, and it was going to eat away at her cousin for a hundred years or longer.

She threw open the last door leading to his cell and stopped. The corridor was crowded. "Move," she commanded, pushing her way through the mass of guards.

Turning the slight bend leading to his cell, she stopped in her tracks. The door was open wide, keys hanging from the lock. Fuil knelt at the floor, his hands holding the chain that had been around Talin's neck.

He looked up at her, anger in his eyes. "Leave us!" he commanded.

The guards brushed past her, not caring who she was, and headed to the exit.

Cautiously, she moved to the door as he rose. "Where's Talin?"

"Gone."

"How? When?" Panic rose in her throat.

Fuil leveled a piercing gaze at her, "I was hoping you could tell me."

She leaned against the opening. "He was here, chained, when I was finished with him. I saw the guard lock the door and hang the keys up before I left."

"You didn't come back?"

She shook her head. "No. I returned to my room, got something to eat. Slept. This is the first time I've been down here today." She swallowed. "When was he discovered missing?"

"Two hours ago, when they brought him something to eat. I need him alive, Iris." He moved closer, towering over her. "I don't give a damn about whatever vendetta you have with Keryth's Successor. I only let you have access to him because it amused me to do so. And, from what the guards told me, your methods of 'torture' are unorthodox but left him weakened in some ways. When I find him, though, you are to stay away. My plans are far more integral than your petty revenge."

"I can help search…" She backed away from him, fear taking hold.

Iris gasped when his hand flew up and grasped her by the chin. His thumb dug into the base of her jaw. "You will go to your room and wait. If you do anything else, I will know." Her body slammed into the wall as he pushed her away.

Knowing better than to argue. She bolted down the hall, fear and panic driving her feet forward.

Chapter Thirteen

Lily splashed water on her face, grateful to wash at least some of the dirt from the ride off her face. A full bath was in order, yes, but it wouldn't happen for a while yet. They had rooms, and stable space for their horses. She was hungry, though, and knew Rylin was as well. Food first.

"It smelled good downstairs," Rylin said. "They might have something we can eat for a late lunch. Soon as you're ready, I'll get Kade and we can go down."

Lily turned, scowling. "He can eat alone as far as I'm concerned. Or I will." She picked up a towel and scrubbed at the drops of water on her hands.

"Lily," Rylin sighed, "how long are you going to keep punishing him? You haven't said a word to him since we got on the road five days ago! He didn't have a choice about leaving Talin there."

"He shouldn't have taken him there to begin with!" She threw the towel back on the bureau. "It's just…I can't find him, Rylin! I can't feel Talin through our link. It's like he's cut me off from his thoughts." She sank into a chair, fear and worry bubbling to the surface. "As far as we know," she swiped at a tear that ran unchecked down her cheek, "he's dead."

Her friend knelt in front of her and took both of her hands in her own. "He's not, Lily. You heard the message yourself. Fuil wants to use Talin to force your mother's hand. He won't be killed."

"Not yet, anyway. I mean, when she meets up with him, what guarantee do we have that he won't execute him right in front of her?"

Rylin placed both hands on Lily's head and forced her to look at her. "I won't lie to you, Lily. That's a possibility. But I know your mother enough that she's got another plan in her head. She won't sacrifice Talin. We need to get the proof she needs, that he's not part Danaan, and then we'll meet with her. Queen Keryth's one of the most skilled politicians I've ever met. I should know. My mother was constantly playing that game. But she could never beat your mom. And Kade feels horrible. Even without you giving him the silent treatment. He and Talin have been best friends longer than either one can remember. Do you think he would've left him there willingly?"

Lily sniffed and shook her head, conceding. Rylin was right. Kade and Talin had been, from all she'd seen and heard, inseparable their entire lives. Given how protective both were of her, she could imagine how hard it must've been for him to leave Talin behind.

"Come on," Rylin said, rising. "Let's eat so we can start asking questions. The sooner we track down his family, the better."

She got up from the chair, swiping at the few tears that still flowed. Her stomach grumbled. A hot meal would be nice.

Kade was standing outside the door as Rylin opened it. Lily sighed. At some point, she'd have to get Rylin to help her, distract him somehow. His constant presence right now rankled her.

She brushed past him and headed downstairs. She wasn't sure what to say to either of them, to be honest. Ever since they'd come into view of Isanne's Well, she'd been feeling restless. Antsy. *Well, why not? Your fiancée's gone missing, taken prisoner by a race straight out of mythology. Heren came back and tried to assassinate your parents. And Mom sent you off on some silly little trip to get you out of the way while she tries to prevent a war. Instead of helping, you're stuck trying to find out who Talin's father really was.*

She knew she wasn't acting right, but really didn't care. As they walked down the stairs and into the common room, she muttered, "At least I don't have to worry about paparazzi here."

Rylin threw a puzzled look back at her. "What's that?"

"Huh? Oh, nothing. Just something that used to happen where I was raised. It's hard to explain." She laughed, the sound hollow in her own ears. "But it's something I'm glad doesn't exist here in Tiadar."

Entering the main room, she followed Kade as he made his way to an empty table. "Try to imagine people who invaded every part of your life and said it was their job to do so." She pulled out a chair and sat down.

"Lily, sometimes I wonder about your world."

Lily shrugged. "You're not the only one. I have no intention of going back there, that's for sure."

Kade spoke up. "I'll go get some food for us."

"I hate to say this, but the more you tell me about that world, the more it frightens me. Is there anything from there you miss?" Rylin asked.

"Blue jeans, t-shirts, and sneakers." Lily laughed.

Kade smiled as he sat across from her, "It couldn't be all bad. After all, you survived living there."

Lily glared at him, "Only because I didn't know anything different."

She saw him wince with her words, the tone she used. Her mood soured and the restless feeling returned.

"So," Rylin spoke, her tone seemed forced. "What's the plan? To find Talin's relatives?"

A bowl of stew was placed before her, followed by a basket of bread set in the center of the table. They all fell silent until the server left.

"I figured we'd walk around, talk to the locals. Maybe do some shopping." Kade dipped a roll into his stew. "This is where his mom was from. There's got to be someone who remembers her."

Try as she might, Lily couldn't shake the feeling that Kade's way wasn't going to work. But, until she could come up with something else, she stayed quiet.

They finished their meal and rose. "We're not going to find out anything sitting here," she muttered. Without bothering to see if they followed, she strode to the door and yanked it open.

An older man stood there, surprised. His white hair, thin and windblown, stuck out at odd angles. "Pardon, my lady," he said as he moved aside.

Lily smiled. "My fault, really." She stepped past him and turned to her right. Shop signs lined the path. Picking one at random, she strode past the stable gate and toward the shop.

***

Talin helped the stable hand to unhitch the horses and get them settled in. Myrena sat in the back of the wagon, waiting.

When they were done, he came around and lifted her down to the ground. "Let's go find Tennet," he told her as they walked to the side door of the inn.

The common room was warm and well lit. The wind on the ride into town had a chill to it. The first frost of winter wasn't far off. Talin hoped he could find out where the royal family was at and get there before that happened.

Tennet walked away from the bar, followed by a young lady. "Myrena, this is Irene. She's going to help you clean up and get a new dress."

Talin met Myrena's concerned gaze and smiled at her, "It's fine. Go ahead. I'm sure she'll bring you back when you're done."

"Okay," she replied and disappeared through a door with Irene.

"Thank you for arranging that, Tennet. I hadn't thought of what she might need beyond food."

Tennet shrugged, "I looked around the house, didn't have any clothes that would've fit her. Irene's got several younger sisters. She'll find something suitable. It'll be a damn sight better than the rags she's wearing now." He placed a key in Talin's hand. "Got a room for you and Myrena, then one for myself. Even arranged for a bath and new clothes for you. You're more muscular than I ever was, but I've got some girth on you. Can't have you wandering about looking like that."

He smiled, "Thank you. I know you don't think so, but I owe you. A lot."

"Do yourself a favor, son. When you get back to her, tell her everything. I know you don't want to," he held up a hand, silencing Talin's protest before he could utter it. "I know some of what happened. Wormed it out of Myrena. If Lily's half the woman you say she is, she'll understand. Use that link you two share if you want to. But she's gotta know what happened. Otherwise, it'll drive a wedge between the two of you. And I reckon that's exactly what the wench that did that to you wants."

Talin kept his head low. "I know what you're saying. And part of me agrees with it, but…"

Tennet clasped a hand on Talin's shoulder, "Wasn't anything that happened your fault, Talin. You fought the best you could, but that wench cheated. Don't let your pride get in the way of your relationship." He paused, "Truth be told, that's what destroyed the one between me and your mother. I thought some peddler man wasn't good enough for *my* daughter. Didn't see that it wasn't about me, but her. Don't make my mistake."

Looking up, he met Tennet's gaze. Saw the pain, regret, in his eyes. "I'll try not to."

"Get going, before that bath gets cold. I'm going to look up an old friend or two. If I don't see you before the morning, I'll at least say goodbye before I leave."

Talin nodded and headed upstairs.

The key in his hand had a scrap of fabric tied to the end with his room number on it. He found the right door and unlocked it. Once inside, he sighed. The room wasn't grand, but there were two beds. A copper tub sat close to the fireplace, stealing warmth. Realizing he probably didn't have much time before Myrena came back, he stripped down and stepped into the steaming water.

His mind went blank as the muscles in his body finally started to relax. Once the water started to turn cool, he got out and found a towel nearby. He'd just finished getting dressed when the latch to his door moved.

Turning, he saw Myrena peek her head in. "Talin?"

"Hey, you're back!"

She came walking into the room, her face beaming. Proudly, she spun and showed off the dress and apron she now wore. "Do you like it?"

"You look beautiful. Are you hungry?"

"Not really. Irene gave me some soup and bread. Said we needed to give you time to clean up, too." She skipped over to one of the beds. "Which one's mine?"

"Whichever you want. I'm not picky."

Throwing herself onto one, she called out, "I want this one!"

"Then that's where you'll sleep."

"Talin?"

"Yes?" he answered as he walked around the room, lighting a couple of candles. Night was falling fast.

"How long are we staying here? Is Lily here or do we have to go someplace else?"

"She's not here. I wish she was, but I don't think so. We'll stay for a least two nights. I've got to find out where she might be and get us a horse that's strong enough to get us there."

"Doesn't she have a home?"

"She's got several, actually. She's a princess, after all." He sat down on the other bed.

"A real princess?" Myrena gasped. "Does that mean you're a prince?"

Talin chuckled, "I guess it does. Or, at least, I will be once we're married."

"What's one of her houses like?"

Talin started to describe Lyvanna Keep. "It's not a big house, really. But there's a garden with a maze made out of bushes. And a pond where ducks live." He paused, looking at her. Myrena had drifted off.

Rising, he unfolded a blanket that sat at the foot of her bed and covered her small form with it. He yawned. Food could wait, he decided, and crawled into bed.

***

Lily tossed in bed, the restless feeling refusing to let her sleep. Finally, she gave up and threw the covers off. Glancing over, she saw Rylin's chest rise and fall. *At least she can sleep*, she thought.

She tiptoed to the door. It was late, but maybe someone was still up downstairs who could make her some tea. Anything to calm her down enough to sleep.

Lily slid out the door, closing it quietly behind her, and started to walk, barefoot, toward the stairs. Her hand was on the rail when she heard a door open behind her.

"Lily," Rylin whispered insistently. "Where are you going?"

"I can't sleep," she said, moving down the stairs. "I'm just going to get some tea. Go back to bed."

She heard Rylin moving to catch up with her. Ignoring her friend, she kept heading down the stairs. "Will you just go back to bed? I don't need someone to watch me drink tea."

Turning on the short landing, she descended the last few steps into the common room. A lone figure sat by the fireplace.

"Oh, I'm sorry," she stammered. "I didn't mean to disturb you. I was just..." she stopped, stunned, as the person rose from the chair and moved into better lighting.

"Talin?" she gasped. The restlessness left her and she ran to him, laughing and crying at the same time.

He scooped her up into his arms. "Lily," he whispered.

The feel of his arms around her made all the irritation she'd felt melt away. He was alive! Safe! She pulled back slightly, her fingers gently stroking his cheek. "Kade told me what happened, how you were taken prisoner. I don't know how you escaped, but seeing you here is the best thing I've ever seen." Stretching up, she kissed him.

He broke it off and pulled her close once again. His heartbeat echoed her own. "The whole time, all I could think of was getting back to you."

"How, Talin? How'd you get out of there?" She looked up at him.

The edges of his mouth curled up, "I had help. I—"

"Lily, step back." Kade commanded.

Turning, she stared at her brother. "Kade, it's Talin! What's wrong with you?"

"It looks like him, yes. But Heren tried that once, too. I need to make sure it's him."

"And how do you plan on doing that? Are you going to torture him?" She pointed at the rapier his hand rested on.

"The link," Rylin chimed in.

"What?" Lily asked.

"She wants me and you to use our link, Lily," Talin answered. "Only the real Talin would share that with you. Am I right? Will that satisfy you, Kade?"

Kade nodded, "Yes, it would."

Lily turned back to Talin, "Well, that's easy enough to do." She opened her mind and reached out for his.

He was Talin, all right, but something was different. There was part of him that he wasn't letting her see. Breaking off the link, she stepped away.

"Lily?" Kade asked.

"It's him," She lowered her voice. "But you're not letting me see everything. There's a gap in your memory, someplace you won't let me go. What's wrong, Talin? What are you hiding?"

He slumped onto a bench. "Please, Lily. Don't ask me that."

She sat next to him. "You promised me you'd never hide any part of your mind from me. What happened? I need to know."

He raised his head and looked at her. The firelight made shadows dance across his face, but she could read the fear, the pain. "I don't want to hurt you, Lily."

"Then let me see what happened."

He stared at her, not saying a word. Finally, he nodded once.

She reached out with her mind and found his. The memories swirled around. A blow to his jaw, waking up chained. All of that she'd seen when he first let her in his mind.

And then Iris came into the room.

Bile rose in her throat as the memory moved forward. She felt Talin go through the same fear she herself had when Heren had made similar threats to her. Only, Iris carried them out. She severed the link and gently brushed aside the tear she saw on his face. "I'm so sorry," she whispered. "No one should ever go through something like that."

"You're not mad?"

"At Iris, yes." Lily surprised how calm she sounded. Inwardly, the rage was barely held in check. That Iris would hate her so much to do that…to Talin, to her. Right now, though, Talin needed her. She turned, ready to say something to Kade, only to find he and Rylin had left the room. Facing Talin again, she continued, “You didn’t want that to happen, and it’s not going to have the effect on me she thought it would. I love you, Talin. And I know you love me. She’s never going to convince me otherwise.”

Leaning in, she kissed him and then let her head rest against his chest. “You’re home now. That’s what matters.”

Chapter Fourteen

Talin woke, relief flooding through him. After finding Lily the night before, and her reaction to what he'd been through, he felt like a weight had been lifted from his shoulders. One he didn't realize he carried.

They'd stayed up for a bit longer, simply enjoying the time alone. She'd filled him in on what had happened to her. He told her about Myrena and his grandfather. Only when both of them were exhausted did they go back to their rooms.

Myrena stirred and he turned toward her bed. "Good morning," he said.

"I'm tired," she whined, rolling over.

"I have a surprise for you."

She flipped back over, eyes wide open. "What is it?"

Rising, he moved over to her bed and sat down next to her. "Would you believe Lily's here? In a room right across the hall?"

Myrena's jaw dropped. "Really? How'd she get here? You said she was somewhere else."

"She was trying to find my family. Instead, she found me."

Chewing her bottom lip, she asked, "Does she have stuff to make hot chocolate?"

Talin laughed. "I'm not certain, but it wouldn't surprise me. Come on, then," he stood up. "Get dressed and brush your hair. I told her about you last night, how you helped me escape. She wants to meet you."

A few minutes later, he led her out of the room and knocked on the door across from theirs.

It swung open and Rylin smiled at him. "Talin, good morning! This must be Myrena? Lily told me about her."

"Myrena, this is Rylin. She's one of Lily's best friends." He smiled as the girl suddenly got shy and tried to hide behind him.

"Come in," Rylin invited them both. "Lily's talking with Kade, *finally*, but she'll be right back."

Talin led Myrena into the room. "Why did you say 'finally' like that? Is there a problem I don't know about?"

"Not really. Well, not anymore." She sat down and gestured to a couple of other seats. "She blamed him for leaving you behind, for taking you there in the first place. She knew it was wrong of her to do so, but she was scared. Her anger and fear had to be directed at someone."

"And now that I'm free, she's talking to him again?"

"Yes." She paused, "Talin, I don't know what you shared with Lily last night. I don't want to know. But she was so angry this morning. Kept muttering things about Iris was going to pay. When Kade came by, she sprung on him. Demanded that they talk alone. She's barely said two civil words to him in the last few days, so he didn't question it."

He ran a hand through his red hair. He wasn't concerned that Lily would give Kade details of how Iris treated him. It was Iris' presence that gave him the most concern. If she'd been colluding with the elves in some way, it was possible that she'd handed Fuil information about Keryth that would help him during any battle ahead of them. "Iris was there, Rylin. In the mountain with the Danaans. And she wasn't being held hostage like I was. Most likely, they're hatching the best way to let Keryth know. Finding her there was…not expected."

Rylin nodded, "It wouldn't surprise me. She's their cousin, yes. But I fear Iris has destroyed any bridge that might bring her back to them."

"She didn't simply destroy it, Rylin. She obliterated it," Lily said as she walked into the room.

Talin rose and looked past Lily to Kade. His friend's face was filled with anger and regret. "I get first shot at her. Only person I'll give way for is your mother."

Kade met his stare, "You've earned it." He paused, "Talin, I'm—"

"Not responsible for a damn thing that's happened to me. Got it? If anything, you made it so I could find my mother's family. And Myrena." He turned and smiled at his rescuer. Holding out his hand, he motioned for her to come forward and take it. "Lily, this is Myrena. She's the reason I got out of there. I made her two promises in exchange for her aid. One was to meet you."

Lily smiled at her, "And I'm very happy to meet you, Myrena. I'm in your debt for taking care of Talin for me." She glanced up at Talin. "What was the other promise?"

"I told her you'd make her some hot chocolate."

"As much as I could drink!" Myrena insisted, stomping her foot.

Talin joined with his friends as they laughed. It felt good to do that, be with them again. "Of course!" Lily rose and headed to her pack. Rummaging around, she pulled a small box out. "Kade, could you let the innkeeper know I need a mug full of warm milk?"

"Sure," he replied and left the room.

Talin sat down, watching how Myrena was in awe of Lily. Truth be told, he was as well. He could tell she was angry. It was little things that gave it away. The way she flexed her hands, moved her head from side to side.

I'm not angry with you, Talin.

I know, he thought back at her. *But I don't want you to be consumed with revenge, either. That's what got Iris where she's at.*

Soon as she's dead, it ends. I promise.

Lily, what if...what if she got what she wanted already?

She froze and shot a terrified look at him.

"What's wrong?" Myrena asked her.

She smiled and Talin saw her look back down. "Nothing, Myrena. Can you tell me where you're from while we wait for the milk? I can't make the hot chocolate without it."

He put a hand to his head, rubbing at his temple, while Lily and Myrena talked. He hadn't really expected an answer from her. He certainly didn't know what to do if Iris had gotten her way.

We cross that bridge when we come to it. I know Mom will want her taken alive if at all possible. But that may not happen. Besides, she may not be able to have a child.

Talin started. That was a situation he hadn't considered.

The door opened again and Kade entered, holding two mugs of milk. Tennet followed behind him, shutting the door.

Rising, Talin crossed the room to his grandfather as Kade set the mugs down on a small table near Lily. "I see you met Kade," he said.

Tennet smiled. "Aye. Found him in the hallway as I was waiting for you to answer my knock. Told me you and Myrena were over here." He bowed toward Lily. "Forgive me, Your Royal Highness. Should've greeted you proper when I entered the room."

Talin smiled and turned toward where she stood, mixing the drinks. "Lily, this is my Grandfather, Tennet. If it wasn't for him and Myrena…"

Lily beamed at the two. "No need to stand on ceremony here, Tennet. I'm glad to meet you. I have a favor to ask you, though. I hate to do it…you've done so much already. Finding Talin, helping him recuperate—"

"Was my honor, Princess. Didn't know right off when the little lass there led me to him, that he was family.

Wouldn't have mattered anyhow. Not about to leave someone stranded where those creatures could get their claws into them." He nodded. "Whatever you need from me, it's yours."

She handed Myrena a mug and watched the girl take a seat. "I know Talin made promises to her. And I'd gladly help him fulfill them. But where we go next isn't a place for a young girl to be."

"You want me to watch over her until the war's won, is that it?"

Lily blinked, "Well, yes. If you can. It's just—"

"Don't need to know the reasons, lass. Pretty much told Talin the same thing last night, when we arrived. I'll take her home with me until you're ready for her to come visit."

"This is good!" Myrena exclaimed. Her hands clasped the mug as if it was solid gold.

Talin joined in with his friends as they laughed. "Now, you might have to tell me what goes into this magic drink of yours. Else it'll be a long winter." Tennet said.

Talin leaned back in the chair, relaxing for a brief moment. How long ago had they been able to sit around like this, making jokes or just talking with each other? He knew it wasn't that long ago, but it felt like it had been. Given what was going to happen in the near future, who knew when he'd be able to relax again. Right now, he just wanted to enjoy the calm.

"Talin? Do I really have to go with Tennet?" Myrena interrupted his thoughts.

He leaned forward and looked at her. "Yes, I think so. He'll be able to keep you safe all winter. Where we have to go next—" he waved around the room "—isn't going to be safe. Not at first. I promise, Lily and I will let Tennet know when it's okay."

Her eyes filled with tears and her lower lip trembled.

"Myrena, it's going to be okay. I promised you that you'd get to meet Lily and have hot chocolate, right?" She nodded her head. "I keep my promises. Lily gave Tennet some powder so he can make you hot chocolate. As soon as this is over, we'll let you come."

Before he knew it, she was flying into his arms. He returned her hug and whispered, "Don't worry. It's going to be fine. You'll be at one of the palaces before you know it."

She pulled away, sniffing. "Okay," she whispered, "but only because you promised."

"Come on, child. I've got to get a few extra supplies to make sure you and I have a comfortable winter." Tennet held out his hand and Myrena went to take it. "Take care of yourself, all of you. I'll await your word." With that, he turned around and left the room, Myrena in tow.

Talin stood as they left, his heart heavy. Lily's arms encircled his waist. "They'll be fine, Talin. Both of them. I have no doubt you'll see them again."

He nodded and replied, "I hope you're right."

"When I was getting the milk, I got a horse for you, Talin. And asked the innkeeper to have ours saddled and ready. We need to get moving." Kade said.

Talin turned, "Where to, Kade? The Queen's got to be on the move toward the meeting with Fuil by now."

"Lily and I sent a message to her this morning, letting her know you were safe. We told her about Iris, your grandfather, as much as we felt she needed to know to best serve her negotiators. She's mobilized all the forces she can and they're converging on a valley. The same one I staggered out of the mountain and into when I was released. Fuil didn't tell her where to meet him, just that she was to do so. She picked the field of battle."

"How many days on the road are we looking at?" Talin asked.

"If we ride hard, we can be there in under a week." Kade took a breath. "Just in time for the fun to begin."

Lily moved away from Talin. "Go pack, both of you. Rylin and I have to change and do the same. We'll meet you in the stables."

"Lily, that's not what Mom told you this morning. She told you to stay as far away from the battle as you could."

"No, Kade. I won't. I spent most of my life hiding. No more. I'm the Successor. I can't sit out a battle."

Kade glared at her, "And that's why you should, Lily! If something goes wrong, if the Queen falls—"

Talin saw Lily draw herself up tall, staring down her brother. The strength he'd seen in her was finally coming out. "Then I will be there to rally the troops and remind them that Tiadar is more than one person, one family. I *am* going, Kade. Try and leave me behind and I'll cast a shadrim and beat you there!"

Reaching out, Talin grabbed at Kade's arm. "Come on, Kade. She's made up her mind. And, quite frankly, she outranks you. If she's willing to take on your mother's wrath, so be it." He smiled at Lily. "It should be fun to watch those two figure out who's more stubborn."

He pulled open the door and pushed his friend out into the hallway.

Chapter Fifteen

The ominous chill they'd felt during most of the ride finally delivered on the promise of an early winter. When they finally reached the inn, frost decorated the windows. There'd be snow by morning. Rubbing his hands together briskly, he knelt before the fire in the fireplace of his room. The innkeeper hadn't lit it until they'd arrived.

His breath steamed as he exhaled. It was going to take time for warmth to reach his fingers and toes. Grabbing a chair, he pulled it closer to the fire and sank into it. He could've stayed down in the common room with the others, only he needed some time alone. He needed to think.

Since that first night, Lily hadn't said a word about what Iris did to him. He knew she thought about it. Not through the link. He'd never force his way into her mind. That's what Heren had done to her. But he could see it on her face. Iris had gotten her revenge. Her presence would forever be between the two of them.

He stared blankly at the flames dancing in the fireplace. He could be thinking of Lily, but she'd see Iris.

"No, Talin. I won't." Lily's voice came from behind him.

He twisted in the chair, staring at her. "I…I didn't hear you come in."

She crossed the room, grabbing another chair and pulling it with her. Talin watched her. The riding pants she insisted on wearing hugged her curves, reminding him that his attraction to her went beyond who she was as a person. Physically, he adored every inch of her. Or wanted to.

She set the chair down next to his. Close enough to touch him and not block the warmth of the fire. Leaning back, she leveled a direct look at him. "I know we could do the whole link thing, but I think things need to be said."

She took a deep breath, "Something's not right with you. I know it's not. It's like you're afraid of something you can't even admit to yourself."

"I don't know what—"

"And I think it has to do with what Iris did to you."

He drummed his fingers on the arm of the chair. "I'm okay, really. It's nothing you should—"

"Stop blaming yourself, Talin," she interrupted him. Leaning forward, she grasped one of his hands in hers. "You know what Heren..." she swallowed and looked away. Taking a deep breath, she continued. "You know what Heren planned to do to me. How he threatened to rape Rylin in front of me. If any of that had come to pass, would you have blamed me?"

"No! Of course not!"

"Then why do you think I'd blame you for what Iris did? She drugged you, Talin. Forced herself on you after taking away any chance you had to resist. This was not your fault."

He shifted in his seat, unable to meet her gaze. "I should've fought her off, found a way." His voice trailed off.

"Why? Because you're a man? It doesn't matter." Her hands left his and forced him to look back at her. There was love in her green eyes, compassion. But no blame. "It doesn't matter, Talin. Not to me. What she did was wrong on so many levels. But you and I are stronger than she gives us credit for. We can beat her. Make it so the wedge she hoped to drive between us never forms."

For the first time since Iris walked into his cell, he felt a little bit of hope. "How?" he whispered.

Lily bit her lip and looked away. Her cheeks flushed a deep red. "Well," her voice dropped to barely over a whisper. "I was thinking that it would help if I gave you some good memories to remember."

Talin stared at her for a minute, confused. "We have those now, Lily. I don't know what you mean."

She rose and moved closer to him. He could see her body trembling. "Are you cold?"

She sat in his lap, easing her arm around his back. The other one she rested on his chest. "No," she whispered. "Not cold. Just a little unsure. I've never done this before." She giggled nervously.

"Done what?"

Her mouth closed in on his. There was a determined tenderness to the kiss. He responded in kind, wrapping his arms around her and pulling her body closer to his. She broke away, moving to leave a trail of kisses on his neck. His breath caught in his throat as his body responded to her. "Lily," he whispered, "are you trying to seduce me?"

She raised her head and locked her green eyes with his. "Is it working?"

He put his hand on the back of her head and pulled her closer, Her black hair cascaded around him as he answered her question with a deep kiss of his own.

***

"Talin? You awake? We've got to get on the road soon."

Kade's voice chased sleep out of Talin's mind. "Oh, um…sure. I'll just be a minute," he called out.

He looked down and placed a kiss on Lily's nose. Her fist was in her mouth, but her body shook with suppressed laughter. "I think he's gone," Talin whispered.

She beamed at him. "Good." Throwing the covers off the two of them, she rose and padded over to the pile of clothing. "Best not keep them waiting long."

Rising, he went up behind her and circled her waist with his arms. "I love you," he said.

She spun around, pressing herself against his chest. "I know," she replied. "I love you, too." He bent down to kiss her, but she moved away. “If we do that, we’ll keep Kade waiting all morning,”

“And the weather isn’t going to help.” Talin sighed. *Duty be damned*, he thought. Lily was right. They had to get to the encampment today if they could. Resolutely, he grabbed his trousers off the floor. Moving back to the bed, he pulled them on. Then, he let himself have a moment to watch Lily as she got dressed.

The blush on her cheeks was still present and he found it beautiful. She was right. He needed to replace the memories in his head with good ones.

“What has you smiling?” Lily asked, as she grabbed his shirt off the arm of a chair.

“You,” he said, pulling her closer as she got near enough.

She laughed. Talin held her close, his cheek resting against her abdomen. The fabric of her shirt was only slightly softer than her skin.

“Talin, Lily’s—” Talin whipped his head toward the door as it crashed open. Kade stood there, his face unreadable.

He felt Lily bend down, her hair covering him as she kissed the top of his head. The shirt slid down his back as she let go of it. “I’m going to go find Rylin,” she whispered. Straightening, she turned and walked away.

Talin turned away from the door, grabbing for his shirt. He heard her say something to Kade, and the door shut.

Neither of them spoke. Talin finished getting dressed, rising in order to reach his boots. Unable to stand the silence any longer, he rose and turned to face Kade. “It’s not what you think.”

Kade leaned against the wall, close to the door. A smirk broke across his friend’s face. “Oh? Rylin told me Lily had every intention of seducing you last night. To the point of asking her how to go about it.”

Talin felt his cheeks redden. “Well, maybe it is.” He laughed a little, relieved. “If you knew, why the big entrance?”

“It was going to take too long for you two to get moving if I didn’t. I’m sure Rylin’s got her moving now. By the way, it snowed last night.” He pushed away from the wall and placed a hand on the door latch. “You might want to find the heaviest coat you’ve got.” Opening the door, he left.

Moving quickly, Talin pulled on his coat and unpacked his gloves. He glanced out the frosted window as he reached for his pack. The ground below was covered in a blanket of white. It’d slow them down, but they had to get to the encampment before sundown.

The sun appeared to touch the peak of the Elivin Mountains when they rounded the last bend and the valley came into view. A thousand or more tents spiraled out from a larger complex in the center. At the base of the mountain, barely visible in the fading light, sat a white pavilion with open sides.

Talin pointed to it. “That’s got to be where Fuil plans to meet with Queen Keryth.”

Kade nodded, “You’re probably right. Let’s get down there before it starts.”

Touching his heels to his horse’s flanks, he urged it forward.

The four of them wove their way through the camp toward the royal tent. Runners were sent to alert Keryth of their approach as soon as they got to the perimeter. Several guardsmen came forward, holding their reins as they dismounted. One pushed his hood back.

“Talin, I’m glad you’re safe,” Grayson held out a gloved hand.

He took it, “That makes two of us. Their Majesties?”

"Inside, waiting on you. The elven King is waiting for nightfall before he'll come out and talk."

"That doesn't surprise me." He patted Grayson on the back as he followed Lily and the others into the tent.

Keryth and Corvin stood with advisors around a large table. The Queen turned as they entered. Talin bowed automatically, but caught the flash of anger on her face. It wasn't directed at him.

"Everyone else out. His Majesty and I will speak with these four alone." Her voice was even, as always, but layered with a tone of command from someone who wouldn't be disobeyed.

The tent cleared quickly. "What are you doing here, Lily? I told you to stay away." Keryth said as she sank into a chair.

"I know you did." Lily responded, her back straight.

"You disobeyed an order from your Queen? There'd better be a good reason for it." She leaned forward in the seat. "Tomorrow, there's going to be a battle out there." She gestured toward the tent door. "As my Successor, it's your duty to be ready to take up rule should I not survive the fight!"

"As Successor, it's my duty to keep every Fomorian safe. Make sure they have food and shelter. And that includes my Queen." Lily's voice was even. Talin covered his mouth to hide the smile. Lily was finally getting rid of the last vestiges of what Erena had instilled in her and coming into her own.

Be nice, he sent to her. *She had reasons to keep you safe.*

"Mom," Lily began, "I know what you want. Me to be safe, all of that. But I can't sit this one out. If I'm going to rule when you're gone, I have to know all there is about the job. The closest I've been to battle is watching movies. I have no idea about how to deploy troops, set up a place for the wounded. War happened where I was, yes. But it wasn't like this. What I saw was sanitized, cleaned up. Flag-draped coffins being saluted. If I'm going to have the responsibility of sending them to war, I need to know what that truly means. And I'm not going to learn that by sitting in a garden in a palace." She moved forward and knelt in front of Keryth. "That's why I came. Not because I wanted to be some rebellious girl or in harm's way. But because I *need* to be here."

Nice enough for you? Lily's voice echoed in his mind.

You're learning fast.

Keryth sighed, "I don't like it, but I see your reasoning. One condition. You do not go anywhere near the actual fighting. And remain under guard at all times. If the battle turns against us, I charge the three of you—" she pointed at Talin, Rylin, and Kade "—to make sure she gets away and to safety. Do I make myself clear?"

Talin nodded, "Yes, Your Majesty." The other two joined in with him.

Corvin cleared his throat, "Talin, stay near me. There's things you'll have to learn as well. Though not about warfare."

Keryth snapped her head back and looked at him, but didn't say a word.

The tent flap moved. "Pardon, Your Majesties," Grayson said as he entered, "but…they're heading to the pavilion."

Keryth rose. "Thank you. I'll be out momentarily." Once the guardsman had left, she looked around. "Kade, you and Rylin stay with Lily. I'll take Talin and your father with me."

Talin saw Lily rise and draw breath, but Keryth raised a hand to stop her. "If you must, stay in contact with Talin through your link. But I'm not about to have you at that table. There are other ways to learn diplomacy than to meet with the Danaans."

Be careful, she sent to him. *It wouldn't surprise me if Iris was there.*

If you're there with me, even in my head, she won't win. He sent back.

He fell into step behind Keryth and Corvin. As they left the tent, a score of armored guards surrounded them.

"Talin, I don't want you to say a word when we meet them. Your presence alone will be enough. I know what Iris did to you, and she will pay for it eventually. Talk to Lily, watch, see if you can find any chinks in their armor that we can exploit later on when the fighting happens."

"You don't think they'll go back to the mountain peacefully?"

"No, I don't." She grew quiet for a moment, then continued. "Fuil committed acts of war, Talin. Nothing in what he's done was peaceful. I fully expect this new 'treaty' of theirs will be nothing more than a demand for me to cede power and rule to him."

"Then why talk to him?"

"It's the mental part of the battle," Corvin chimed in. "It's one thing for the Crown to say this is justified, ask the soldiers to lay down their lives. It's another for them to see diplomacy tried and fail. This way, they know all efforts to spare lives were made."

Pay attention, Talin, Lily's thought echoed in his head. *I'm learning with you.*

They cleared the encampment and the perimeter guards. "Your Majesty, I recommend you increase the fires on the edges of the camp before nightfall."

Keryth glanced back at him, "Why?"

"The Danaans have lived in near dark for centuries now. Their sight has adjusted. The brighter the light, the less likely they'll sneak up on you."

"That would explain why we're doing this now, at twilight."

They started to cross the open field. Several people moved in the open pavilion ahead of them. Talin couldn't make them out yet, but his stomach tightened.

She won't beat us, Talin. We're stronger than she is.

He took a deep breath and shook off the momentary fear. *I love you*, he sent back.

I know.

The grass, heavy with frost and a dusting of snow, crunched under his feet. It would make the fighting harder. For both sides.

Ten yards away, he recognized faces. Fuil was there, seated at the center of the table. Chadine and Anstara flanked the back of the chair. Iris sat to his left.

She's here, next to him.

Don't be afraid of her, Talin. She no longer has any power over you.

Fuil rose as the guards parted and let them enter. "Keryth, I'm pleased to finally make your acquaintance." He turned toward Corvin and Talin. "I see both of the Consorts have recovered from their recent trials. That must make you happy."

"What would make me happy, Fuil, is for you to go back to Eire from whence you came. Barring that, into that mountain and abide by the treaty your own mother drafted." Keryth stood, her hands resting on the back of the chair in front of her.

The elven king smiled, but it wasn't a pleasant one. "Oh, no. Never that. My mother was a fool to believe we should be put aside, stay silent. This world is ours by right. Surrender it now, or watch as I slay your family in front of you."

Keryth sighed. "Truly you are not your mother's son. She was a wise woman, with a vision. Tell your Danaan troops to say their goodbyes. When we are done with you, there will be no more of your kind left in Tiadar." She turned and raised her hand, motioning them to follow.

Talin? What happened?

War was declared.

Chapter Sixteen

Talin darted into the tent, grateful for the blast of warmth that greeted him. "The lines are still holding," he reported. "Fuil's forces are trying different spots, looking for a weakness."

Keryth turned from the table. "Show me," she commanded him.

He pulled off his gloves and stuffed them in his pockets. "Here," he pointed at the map, "and here. Those were the last two places they hit. The extra bonfires are helping, but their archers have been finding their mark too often. If we keep reacting and shifting troops every time they attack, Fuil's going to start making us run ourselves to the ground."

"Well," she sighed, "daybreak's less than an hour away. Most likely, they'll retreat back into the mountain. I don't want to take the fight in there if I can help it. They'll have the advantage."

A blast of cold air alerted him, and Talin glanced over his shoulder. Lily walked in, her face weary. Kade wasn't far behind.

"How many wounded, Lily?" Corvin asked, looking up from the map.

Talin draped an arm around her and pulled her close as she approached him. "Hundreds. I sent Rylin to get some sleep. The medics said we couldn't do much good if we couldn't stand up."

Talin studied the board a bit more. He was no strategist, but he knew enough that there was a danger. If the enemy forces could pull enough of their troops to one side, the other would be vulnerable.

"Corvin, no! I forbid it!" Keryth's voice rang out.

Talin looked up. The royal couple were staring each other down. "Keryth, it's the best option we have."

"I will not allow you to—"

Corvin raised a hand, stopping her protest. "It's not your decision to make, my Queen. It's mine. You gave me the authority the day you asked me to be your consort. It will be done." He turned to Talin. "Go over to our tent. In the bedchamber, under a cot, is an old box. Made of oak and iron, with runes etched into both the wood and the metal. Bring it here. Please."

His arm slid away from Lily. "Of course." He gave Lily's hand a slight squeeze as he left.

The sleeping tents were just a few steps away from the main pavilion they'd been in. Once inside the room, he started looking under the cots. Dropping onto his belly, he was grateful that there was a thick rug between him and the floor of the tent. Even with the extra layer, he started to feel the cold seep up from the ground and through his pants.

He pushed aside a few boxes and spied the one Corvin had requested. Jerking at the handle on the side, he pulled it out. He lifted it up onto the bed and then picked himself up off the floor.

Lily, he thought, *do you know what's in this box?*

A wave of sadness hit him before she responded. *I do now. And he'll tell you when it's time. I can't.*

Talin took a deep breath. Something had happened while he was gone. Keryth and Corvin kept some things private, and he could respect that. Grasping the chest by the handles, he started to make his way back to the pavilion.

The air was heavy when he walked back in. Kade held Lily. Both had tears leaving streaks on their cheeks. Corvin embraced Keryth, his face held a stoic resolve. He locked his gaze on Talin and nodded once. He gently pushed Keryth away and gave her a kiss before walking over to Kade and Lily. Talin watched him embrace both of his children, whispering something to each of them. A thought struck him. He was watching a man say goodbye to his family. Whatever was in the chest he carried would most likely end Corvin's life.

"Your Majesty, I..." Talin couldn't finish the thought.

"Not now, Talin. And I know what you would say. I'll explain everything before this begins. Follow me."

Talin turned and followed him back out into the cold light of morning.

Corvin waved off his escort. "What will be done needs no witness beyond you," he told Talin.

Talin didn't know what to say. The man he'd looked up to as a father walked like a man about to die. Whatever the reason, it still stung.

He knew better than to try and talk to Lily through their link. Whatever was to happen was for him to see, not her. He couldn't help but send her love, though, and let her know he wanted to be at her side.

They made it to the perimeter fires. "Sergeant," Corvin called out.

A man trotted over to them. "Yes, Your Majesty?"

"Whatever you see or hear, do not leave your post. Do not let your soldiers come out to our side. When we are done, Talin will let you know. Only then can you cross this line." Corvin kept his words crisp.

The Sargent looked at Talin and the chest, then nodded. "As you wish, Your Majesty."

Corvin nodded and stepped out into the field. The frost-covered grass crunched loudly beneath their feet as Talin followed. The meager warmth from the sun wasn't enough to melt the ice.

Halfway between the bonfire line and where the pavilion had been the night before, Corvin stopped. "Here is close enough, I think." His breath steamed in the cold air. "Put the chest down, Talin, with the lock facing the mountain."

Talin knelt, easing the box onto the ground, and spun it as directed. “Shall I open it?”

“No, not yet.” Corvin turned from the mountain and looked at him. “Do you remember your oath, Talin? The one you took at the ceremony?”

Talin furrowed his brow, “I believe so. Why?”

“Tell me them again.”

“I, Talin, ward of House Meagher, do submit to the will of the Successor and become her Consort. I shall rule at her side, support her in all things. I shall hold the wellbeing of all the Fomori within the realm of Tiadar dear and not abide any that would cause them ill. I—”

“Stop,” Corvin interrupted. “What do you think that last line means?”

Talin blinked, “That I will put the safety of every citizen, no matter age or station, as sacred and defend them against all foes.”

Corvin nodded, “And if that foe is Lily?”

“Lily’s not going to hurt anyone. I don’t understand what you mean.”

“What if you had the means,” he glanced at the chest, “to end a war? To prevent the needless deaths of hundreds if not thousands of Fomorians, even if it meant your own death, but Lily forbid you from using that power? Would you defy your Queen, the woman you love, and sacrifice yourself to save others?”

Talin met Corvin’s gaze and stood just a little straighter. “Yes, I would.”

Corvin nodded, “I know you would. That day is not today. Not for you, anyway.” He let out a deep breath. “When the exodus happened, Aeowolf was not King. He was the Successor. Balor was on the throne. And he was afraid that the Tuatha would not honor the treaty forever. In the battle that covered the shadrims being cast, Balor was cut down. He was brought through with the rest of us, and gave us a gift before he died. That is what’s in this chest.”

"What is it?"

"His head."

Talin started. "And this will help us how?"

Corvin knelt in front of the box, running his hands over the lid. "Balor was a giant of a man, and I don't mean figuratively. And he possessed great magic. As payment, he gave up one of his eyes. When I uncover it, his magic will be unleashed. Providing I can convince him to do so."

"You're going to summon his spirit? To what end?"

"We all pay a price to use magic, Talin. You know this. But Balor's dead. He can't wield it himself, or pay the cost. Therefore, I plan to do it for him." He threw up the hasp and opened the lid.

Nestled in a bed of faded blue velvet was an object covered with thick linen. It was twice the size of Corvin's head.

Corvin looked back up at Talin. "Remember these words if you can. If not, there's a notebook in my library that will give you the words and more. Things the Consort should know. I pray you never have to do this." He stood and began to speak:

Crom Cruach, hear me now—
The Consort calls to Balor.
Your might is needed, the foe at hand—
Fomorian blood shall be spilled no more.

The wind swirled, kicking up the snow and enveloping them in a tempest of white. The air coalesced into a ghostly form.

"Who summons me?" the spirit demanded.

"I do, Balor. I am Corvin, Consort to the Queen. I ask that you aid us now. The doom you foresaw when we came to Tiadar has come to pass. The Tuatha de Danaan seek to slaughter and enslave us once again. I offer myself as payment for this aid."

The figure sighed, the sound echoing in Talin's soul. "I did fear this would come to pass. Uncloak my eye, Consort, and let my wrath loose. No drop of elvish blood will remain."

Talin's heart stopped. Myrena was part Danaan! Stepping around the chest, he faced the long-dead King. "They are not all evil, Balor. There are some, children who were born from a merging of Danaan and Fomorian, that are innocent. Would you grant them the chance to live?"

The giant turned his head and the full weight of his gaze fell on Talin. Adrenaline surged through his body, but Talin held his ground. "You are Consort, as well. Both compassion and strength live within you. Your Queen will need both from you, for a very long time. Very well. I will see the soul of these Danaan. If they hold no hatred for our kind, they will live."

Talin bowed, "Thank you."

Corvin knelt in front of the chest again. "Talin, get behind the chest again. Now." He reached forward and began to remove the linen wrappings.

Talin moved as he was told. As the head was uncovered, he felt the temperature increase. The ground beneath the chest melted, then began to steam as the grass turned brown from the heat.

"Talin, remind them I loved them. Please." Corvin looked at him and pulled the final piece of fabric free.

A bright light erupted from the Eye of Balor, shooting in uncountable rays toward the mountain. Talin turned away, unable to withstand the ever-increasing glow. Then, the screams began as the beams of light found their prey. The sound echoed out of the mountain and cascaded into the valley.

The wailing subsided, and the glow diminished. Talin opened his eyes and turned back toward the mountain. The chest sat, closed. Corvin, Consort to Queen Keryth, lay on the ground. His chest wasn't moving.

Talin circled around and knelt by the man's body. Tears fell from his eyes as he mourned his passing. He glanced back at the encampment. Soldiers had gathered at the closest bonfire, wondering at what had happened. Rising, he called out, "King Corvin, Consort of Queen Keryth, has given his all to spare Fomorian lives. Who will help me honor him and return his body to the Queen?"

Twenty men came forward, moving at a stately pace. There was no need to rush now. They lifted the body as Talin picked the chest up. He then led them back through the camp to the command pavilion.

Everyone knelt as they passed, mourning their fallen king, then fell into the procession. Talin kept his face calm, trying not to give in to the grief he felt. Spying Grayson, he stopped long enough to hold out the chest. "Put this in my tent, please." Grayson nodded and took it from his hands. Talin led the procession forward again.

Keryth stood at the entrance to the pavilion, with Lily and Kade at each side. Dropping to one knee, he knelt in front of her. "Your Consort has fallen, Your Majesty. And the foe has been defeated."

"Then tonight we shall send him on his way to the Otherworld as befits his station. We shall toast his name, celebrate his bravery, and grieve his passing. So mote it be."

"So mote it be," Talin said. The sound of the troops echoing his words rippled outward to the edges of the encampment.

Chapter Seventeen

The funeral pyre for Corvin was lit. Talin kept his arm around Lily as he watched the smoke and flames reach up and send the man's soul to the stars above.

Tomorrow would be a long day. Keryth had ordered them to go into the mountain and pull out the bodies of the Danaans. And, more specifically, find Fuil and Iris. Talin understood. They all wanted to make sure those two were dead.

"Talin," Keryth kept her eyes on the scene in front of her, "I sent a messenger to your grandfather's homestead. To invite him and Myrena both to Lyvanna Keep. But to also make sure she was alive. I know that's who you thought of when you asked Balor for the favor."

"Thank you," he replied. "I know there are more like her, children of both Fomorian and Danaan parents. Do you think we'll find them tomorrow?"

She turned and faced him. The regal bearing of Queen kept her face a mask, but he saw the pain in her eyes. "If they live, we will find them. Give them shelter, and a home with families that will not judge them. Eventually, the taint of Danaan blood will die with them."

"That may take a few generations."

"Or not. It was rumored, back on Eire, that the children born to such a pairing were sterile. At least, the ones that appeared Fomorian." She put a hand on his arm. "Lily told me what Iris did to you, Talin. And it wouldn't have worked. Her mother was the one Kronos asked Corvin to take away, not yours. Jasper said she was his, but I had my doubts."

Relief flooded through his body, at least for a few minutes. He let out a long breath, the steam dissipating quickly. "Is that why you want her body found?"

"That, and to give her a proper sending. Despite what she did, she was still my niece. I swore, after her parents were slaughtered, to raise her as my own. She made her own choices, but she was still family." She looked back to the pyre. Corvin's body was a dark outline resting on the top, obscured by the flames. "His soul is gone, but the work still needs doing. I will sleep alone tonight, and mourn his passing. Don't let Lily go through that without help."

Tightening his arm around Lily, he nodded. "I won't."

An honor guard stood around the fire, remaining vigilant, while the rest of the encampment slowly moved away. Keryth was right. There was still work to be done. And they couldn't do it without sleep.

He waited until he felt Lily shift before he moved. "It's strange, Talin. I only knew him for a few months, really. But I don't know what I'll do now that he's gone."

He pulled her closer to him, wrapping both arms around her. Her body trembled from grief or cold, possibly both. "You'll get up, get dressed, and do what needs to be done. It'll take time. And some days will have you crippled with grief and wanting him back. Somehow, those days get fewer and farther between. You'll laugh again, and start to remember not how he died but how he lived. The way he laughed, or even how he scolded you. And how much he loved you."

She pulled away, looking up at him. Tears flowed from her eyes. "Is that how you got though this, when your mom died?"

"Yeah," he told her. "It's not easy. But I don't think it's supposed to be." He swiped at a tear as it trickled down her face. "Come on," he whispered, "let's get you someplace warmer."

Together, they walked back toward the command pavilion.

***

Three days later, they still were pulling bodies from the mountain. A handful of survivors were located, young children who didn't have a real home in the Danaan society. The ground, too frozen to dig graves, became littered with pyres.

Talin sat in the tent, his mind numb. So much death surrounded them. The war had been won, but at a high cost. It truly surprised him that so many had hated his race.

"That cut both ways, you know." Kade looked up from the battle map. He reached out and picked up another group of figures, placing them in a box. "You weren't exactly open to friendly relations with them when I first told you."

Talin nodded, "You're right. I suppose the hatred ran deep on both sides. It shouldn't have, though."

"That's the difference, Talin. You know better. Probably changed your view on it now that your rescue depended on someone who was part elf. What about the rest of Tiadar, though? Is it enough to say 'our enemy is dead'?" Kade paused. "Or do we continue to hate anyone that shows up that isn't Fomorian? There's areas we've never explored. I don't think we're alone on this world."

"We offer friendship first, Kade," Lily spoke as she walked into the tent. "Where I was raised, there were problems. Lots of people couldn't accept others because of the color of their skin or what god they prayed to. It caused a lot of violence. I'd rather talk to someone like they're a friend over fear them."

"Unless, of course, there's an army showing up with them." Keryth chimed in. "Extending a hand in friendship is fine. But not if they've been burning and looting on the way to you."

The tent flap moved aside again, drawing Talin's attention. It was Grayson. "Pardon the interruption, Your Majesty. A runner just came in from the Danaan stronghold. They've swept the city. There was no sign of either Fuil or Iris." He held out a small card. "They found this in the room they believed where Iris stayed."

Keryth took the card from him, turning it over in her hand. Her brow furrowed, "I don't understand what this is."

Talin rose as Lily moved closer to her mother. "That's an appointment card," she said, puzzled. "Where Erena raised me, they handed these out to remind you when you had to see the doctor or such."

Keryth held the card out to her, "This is from that world, then?"

"Yes," she replied as she took it. Flipping it over, she read the back.

A lump formed in his stomach as she looked at him. "It's for a fertility clinic. Near as I can tell, the appointment was less than a week ago." Lily handed the card back to Keryth. "She's been to that world at least once, when she and Kade brought me back here. I can see her going back if it helped her enact her revenge."

"If she had an appointment, then it's possible the two escaped via shadrim to that world." Keryth turned to Grayson. "Start to strike the camp. We're heading back to Lyvanna Keep tonight. Leave enough troops here to finish burning the bodies." Turning back to Lily, she asked, "Do you know where in that world this place was?"

"Yes. I mean, there's an address. But I never went out when I lived there. Erena had us out in the country."

"I'm not going to go looking for trouble," Keryth said. "But it's good to know in case they come back. Go pack." She smiled at Kade. "You need to go tell Rylin. I did tell you I planned to get you two married when this was over. I expect to have a date to announce before we reach the Keep."

***

Two hours later, Talin sat on his horse atop a hill. He looked back at the smoke-filled battlefield and sighed.

What's wrong, Talin? Lily's voice echoed in his head.

So much needless death, and for what? Iris is still out there somewhere.

She can't run forever, Talin. And, if necessary, we will take the fight to her. As long as we love each other, though, she won't win. You do still love me, right?

Until the day I die.

He turned his horse and let the valley fade away behind him.

About the Author

Born in the late 1960's, KateMarie has lived most of her life in the Pacific NW. While she's always been creative, she didn't turn towards writing until 2008. She found a love for the craft. With the encouragement of her husband and two daughters, she started submitting her work to publishers. When she's not taking care of her family, KateMarie enjoys attending events for the Society for Creative Anachronism. The SCA has allowed her to combine both a creative nature and love of history. She currently resides with her family and three cats in what she likes to refer to as "Seattle Suburbia".

You can find KateMarie at the following sites:

Twitter: @DaughterHauk
FaceBook: http://www.facebook.com/pages/KateMarie-Collins/217255151699492
Her blog: http://www.katemariecollins.wordpress.com

Other Titles by KateMarie Collins from Solstice Publishing

Mark of the Successor

Dominated and controlled by an abusive mother. Lily does what she can to enjoy fleeting moments of normality. When a break from school only provides the opportunity for more abuse at home, the sudden appearance of a stranger turns her world even bleaker. Disappearing without a trace, he has left a lingering fear in Lily. His parting words to her mother, "Have her ready to travel tomorrow," is something her mind refuses to accept.

Running away is the only answer. But before Lily can execute her plan, a shimmering portal appears in her room. Along with two strangers who promise to help keep her safe. With time running out, she accepts their offer for escape and accompanies them into a brand new world. A world in which she is the kidnapped daughter of a Queen, and the heir to the throne of Tiadar.

Can she find her own strength to overcome both an abusive past and avoid those who would use her as a means to power?

Guarding Charon

One should always read the fine print...especially with an inheritance from a relative you didn't know existed.

In a rut doesn't even begin to describe Grace's life at 22. Her ex is using his position as a cop to stalk her, getting her fired from every job she finds. Her parents, not knowing how abusive he could be, believe all her problems would vanish if she'd simply marry him.

After losing yet another job, a lawyer arrives. A relative has died and left her entire estate in Maine to Grace. Eager to shake the dust of Bruce and small town Texas off of her for good, she leaps at the chance. She even changes her name.

Then she learns that her great aunt was a Witch...and the house has some big secrets. Secrets that she has to protect for six months if she hopes to inherit the entire estate and truly be free of her past.

Arine's Sanctuary

The Moreja Sisterhood exists to rescue boys from abuse and arranged marriages. Arine's on assignment, bringing Cavon back to her home in Sanctuary, when she discovers something terrifying.

He can do magic.

When the chance comes up for her to go back out and rescue her own brother, sold off by her mother ten years earlier, Arine eagerly takes the chance. But can she talk him into coming home to Sanctuary with her? And can they get there before the Domine's army, bent on controlling the magic?

CPSIA information can be obtained
at www.ICGtesting.com
Printed in the USA
FSOW01n1020050218
44195FS

9 781625 265067